I0612026

THE STORY OF THE ILIAD

&

THE BATRACHOMYOMACHIA

The Abduction of Helen

R. von Deutsch, Artist

—CLASSICAL STUDIES EDITION—

THE STORY OF THE ILIAD

&

THE BATRACHOMYOMACHIA

HOMER
PRINCE OF POETS

Retold by Rev. A. J. Church

Compiled and Edited by Allison Ellis

Introduction by Tracy Lee Simmons

MOUNT TITANO
winsome

MOUNT TITANO
winsome

Copyright © 2025 by Mount Titano Media

All rights reserved. No part of this book may be reproduced in any form
by any means without written permission from the publisher.
Reviewers may quote brief passages in connection with a review written
for inclusion in a magazine, newspaper, website, or broadcast.

For information about special discounts for bulk purchases, contact:
sales@MountTitanoMedia.com

Published by Mount Titano Winsome
an imprint of Mount Titano Media

Cover:
The Abduction of Helen. By Gavin Hamilton, c. 1770s.
Image Public domain.

Cover design by Sam Torode
Book design by Paul R. Bienvenue

First paperback edition, 2025

ISBN: 979-8-9918463-7-0

CONTENTS

BEFORE WE SET SAIL by Allison Ellis   ix

READING GUIDE by Allison Ellis   xxvii

INTRODUCTION by Tracy Lee Simmons   xxxvii

PART ONE: THE STORY OF THE ILIAD

CHAPTER

I.	Of How the War with Troy Began	5
II.	The Quarrel	7
III.	What Thetis Did for Her Son	15
IV.	The Duel of Paris and Menelaus	19
V.	How the Oath was Broken	27
VI.	The Great Deeds of Diomed	31
VII.	Concerning Other Valiant Deeds	39
VIII.	Of Glaucus and Diomed	45
IX.	Hector and Andromache	51
X.	How Hector and Ajax Fought	63
XI.	The Battle on the Plain	73
XII.	The Repentance of Agamemnon	85
XIII.	The Embassy to Achilles	91
XIV.	The Story of Old Phoenix	101
XV.	The Adventure of Diomed and Ulysses	109
XVI.	The Wounding of the Chiefs	119

XVII. The Battle at the Wall 127

XVIII. The Battle at the Ships 137

XIX. The Deeds and Death of Patroclus 147

XX. The Rousing of Achilles 157

XXI. The Making of the Arms 167

XXII. The Quarrel Ended 173

XXIII. The Battle at the River 177

XXIV. The Slaying of Hector 185

XXV. The Ransoming of Hector 197

XXVI. The End of Troy 205

PART TWO: THE BATRACHOMYOMACHIA

I. THE BATRACHOMYOMACHIA, translated
   by Hugh G. Evelyn-White, 1914 213

II. THE BATRACHOMYOMACHIA, translated
   by William Cowper, 1791 225

III. THE BATRACHOMYOMACHIA, translated
   by George Chapman, 1624 247

Image Citations 267

— BEFORE WE SET SAIL —

Some people will read the *Iliad* only one time, with little understanding or appreciation.

Not we!

We are not just reading the *Iliad*.

We are joining the billions of readers who have traveled back in time with this monumental story for over 2,500 years. We will sail the centuries on a barque of books, and see how this work—as with all great works—ripples through the ages. We will discover how some of our more latter-day ancestors have responded in their own way to the *Iliad*, concluding with three translations of *The Batrachomyomachia*.

But before we journey all the way back to the Trojan War, we will make a brief stop in the year 1816 to look over the shoulders of Charles Cowden Clark, a minor poet, and his friend, the poet John Keats, as they take their first look together at a then 200-year-old book, a now over 400-year-old book—an Elizabethan translation of the works of Homer by George Chapman. We will then read the poem Keats wrote in response just a few hours later, his now famous: "On First Looking into Chapman's Homer." We will also consider a question that strikes all curious readers of the *Iliad*...

Did the Trojan War really happen?

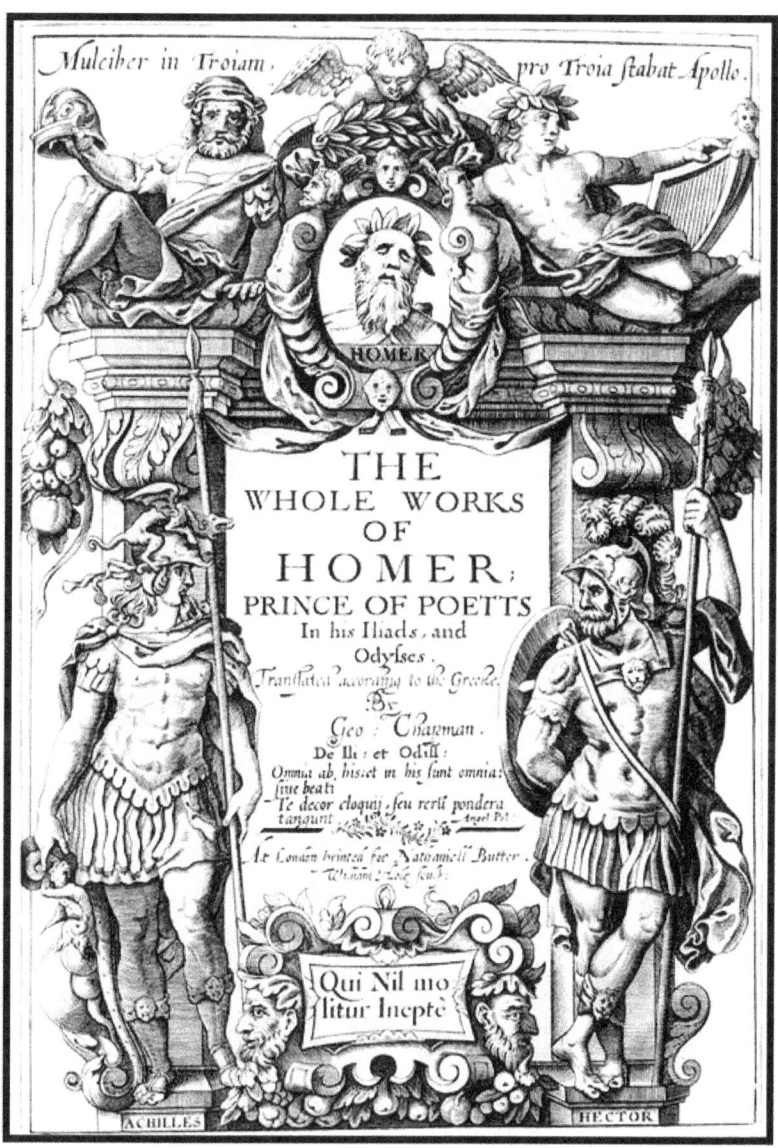

Title Page from Chapman's Translation of Homer, 1616

Chapman's Opening Lines of the *Iliad*
which inspired Keats to compose a poem.

Achilles baneful wrath resound, O Goddess, that imposed
Infinite sorrows on the Greeks, and many brave souls los'd
From breasts heroic; sent them far to that invisible cave
That no light comforts; and their limbs to dogs and vultures gave:
To all which Jove's will gave effect; from whom first strife begun
Betwixt Atrides, king of men, and Thetis' godlike son.

The Original Ancient Greek:

μῆνιν ἄειδε θεὰ Πηληϊάδεω Ἀχιλῆος οὐλομένην
ἣ μυρί᾿ Ἀχαιοῖς ἄλγε᾿ ἔθηκε
πολλὰς δ᾿ ἰφθίμους ψυχὰς Ἄϊδι προΐαψεν ἡρώων
αὐτοὺς δὲ ἑλώρια τεῦχε κύνεσσιν οἰωνοῖσί τε πᾶσι
Διὸς δ᾿ ἐτελείετο βουλή
ἐξ οὗ δὴ τὰ πρῶτα διαστήτην ἐρίσαντε Ἀτρεΐδης τε ἄναξ
ἀνδρῶν καὶ δῖος Ἀχιλλεύς

"On First Looking into Chapman's Homer"

Much have I travell'd in the realms of gold,
And many goodly states and kingdoms seen;
Round many western islands have I been
Which bards in fealty to Apollo hold.
Oft of one wide expanse had I been told
That deep-brow'd Homer ruled as his demesne;
Yet did I never breathe its pure serene
Till I heard Chapman speak out loud and bold:
Then felt I like some watcher of the skies
When a new planet swims into his ken;
Or like stout Cortez when with eagle eyes
He star'd at the Pacific—and all his men
Look'd at each other with a wild surmise—
Silent, upon a peak in Darien.

by John Keats
1816

Did the Trojan War Really Happen?

While Homer's epic poems are considered mythological, many have believed—and archaeological evidence indicates —that there was indeed a great war in Troy in the late 13th or 12th century B.C. and that the town was destroyed by fire.

Most curious scholars enjoy such stories as that of the Trojan War and contemplate what truth lies within the words, but one man who believed in the truth of the Trojan War was determined to prove it—to discover the very site of Troy itself. He was a German businessman and amateur archae-ologist named **Heinrich Schliemann**, who was so resolved and disciplined that he studied ancient Greek and Latin in preparation for his work; traveled in 1870 to a site called **Hissarlick**, a mound in **Turkey**; dug through many layers of ancient towns (using methods that were destructive and no longer used); and discovered a trove of ancient artifacts that he called **"Priam's Treasure."**

It is now widely accepted that Schliemann did indeed discover the ancient town of Troy (though locals and visitors to the area for centuries had also thought it was the site of the ancient town). You can read more about his life and discovery in his book published in 1881: ***Ilios: City and Country of the Trojans*** (a scholarly work, not simple reading).

An anecdote about Schliemann that Classical studies students in particular will appreciate is of a time when Schliemann was a young man working in a grocery store. Schliemann heard a man enter the store reciting lines of the *Iliad* and was mesmerized by the beautiful sounds. Of that encounter, Schliemann wrote: "From that moment on, I never ceased to pray God that by His grace I might yet have the happiness of learning Greek." [1]

---

[1] *Schliemann: The Story of a Gold Seeker*. Emil Ludwig. Boston: Little, Brown, and Company, 1931. Editor's Note: Interestingly, this quote is also attributed 250 years earlier to François Fénelon, the private tutor of the grandson of King Louis XIV of France.

Heinrich Schliemann c. 1860

"Mask of Agamemnon," from 1,600 B.C., found by
Heinrich Schliemann in 1876.

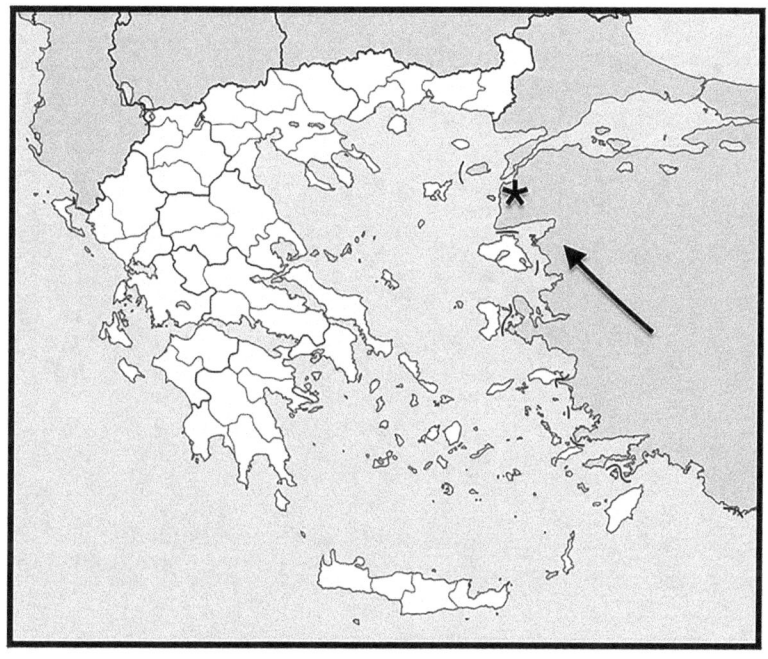

Map of Greece showing site of Ancient Troy in Turkey.

Venetus A: Image from a 10th-century manuscript,
the oldest extant complete copy of the text of the *Iliad*.

Oldest known image of the Trojan Horse, 670 B.C.

MOUNT TITANO MEDIA

CLASSICAL STUDIES EDITION

READING GUIDE

For Individuals and Parents/Teachers Reading with Students

The Art of Translation and *Imitatio*

Homer has been called "the Father of Western Civilization," and we would be hard-pressed to find a great scholar, poet, or playwright, or even a single schoolboy in Ancient Greece and Rome, who did not often read and quote from Homer. Alexander the Great is said to have slept with his treasured copy of Homer's *Iliad* (under his pillow), which was annotated by his tutor Aristotle. Virgil, Dante, Shakespeare, and countless others were inspired and never tired of references and quotes from Homer. The Bible and the works of Homer are the foundational texts of Western Civilization, and they are to be enjoyed over and over throughout life, in various adaptations and translations, and—for those inclined—in the original languages.

We are reading Rev. Alfred J. Church's story of the *Iliad*, a version adapted for first-time (even second- or third-time) readers. We are also reading not one but three translations of *The Batrachomyomachia—The Battle of the Frogs and Mice*—a short parody, or comic epic, of the *Iliad*, traditionally attributed to Homer, though now believed to have been written several centuries later. Why read three translations? A better question might be: Why read *only* three translations? It is for the same reason we read different translations of the *Iliad* or any other great work. There are many ways to translate, and they all offer something different to the reader:

- A **"metaphrase"** is a word-for-word translation and is of greatest benefit to the those studying the grammar and structure of the original language.

- A **"paraphrase"** seeks to capture the essence of the words, and in this instance, the translator's voice comes to the work and the text flows more naturally. This importance of this form of translation cannot be overstated. Readers may read a work and think, "I don't like it," when in fact, it is the translation and not the original that is unsuited to the reader's taste. Tip: If you read a great work in translation and are not attracted to the style, try another translation, perhaps even from another era.

- The third kind of translation—and some debate if it should still be called such—is **"imitation,"** in which the translation does not necessarily stay true to the word choice, sense, or plot. The modern concept of "inspiration" does not include this third type of work, but is supposed to be, in theory, an entirely original creation. However, there is a term in classical rhetoric—*imitatio*—which means composing new works by studying and adapting a work into a new creation that would not be considered original in the modern sense, but is a transformation of the original work (not to be confused with plagiarism). Despite the modern push for "purely original works," it is essentially impossible to find a work without any trace of *imitatio*, and rather than being "bad," that is at the heart of Classical studies. We dedicate decades to reading and making ours the words and thoughts of the greatest artists of all time, and then hopefully come to our wise, informed conclusions, our own inspiration, and our work is a flowering of the fields we have planted in our studies.

The *Batrachomyomachia* falls in the third category, as parody is a specific form of *imitatio*.

British English Spelling & Archaic Diction and Spelling

In this book, you will encounter a few differences in American versus British English spelling of words. For example, "skilful" has been the spelling of the American "skillful" since the Middle English period, first appearing around the 14th century. You will also see words with spelling variation like "gambolled," "harboured," and others which are easy enough to decipher.

It might be natural to think that encountering archaic spelling, British English spelling, and archaic diction will just cause confusion. For this concern, I offer a story:

A friend of mine from Brazil married a man from Mexico, and their child was born in California. They continued to speak their separate mother tongues with their son, and the boy heard English with other family members and friends. When their child was three, he would say sentences along the lines of:

"**Quiero** (Spanish for "I want.") more **leite** (Portuguese for "milk"), Daddy."

My friends were concerned and, after a series of referrals, met with a doctor of childhood development who specialized in language. He advised them to "carry on" exactly as they were, that it was of no concern, and that the child would of his own accord, automatically, separate them over time and speak all three fluently—and that is precisely what happened, and is what happens all around the world when young children are exposed from very young ages to different languages.

To the topic of archaic and British English spelling: If we wish for our children to be able to read books and documents more than 50 or so years old, they will need to be comfortable encountering variations in spelling and diction. Starting with books like this one, where there are only a handful of variations that are easily recognizable, is a perfect way to prepare readers for more challenging texts they will encounter later on. A simple example: Familiarity with the archaic spelling "to-day" and "to-morrow" (which appear throughout this book) will help readers immediately understand the following line spoken in Shakespeare's *Romeo and Juliette*:

"Good night, good night! Parting is such
sweet sorrow,
That I shall say good night till it be
morrow."

and Matthew 6:34 in the King James Bible: "Take therefore no thought for the **morrow**: for the **morrow** shall take thought for the things of itself."

Ideas for Reading in General

Start Early - In general, young children and readers of all ages are capable of far more than we offer and ask of them. It was not unusual, for example, for children in the 19th century to read and enjoy books which many adults today would find challenging. Further, we are accustomed to reading aloud with our children only until they enter preschool or kindergarten, but again looking back to previous centuries, adults read aloud with each other and with their children throughout their lives.

I began reading works written in previous centuries aloud to my child very early. Later, when she was five years old and could be more engaged, we would paraphrase every one or two paragraphs, and we would discuss them until I knew she had a general understanding before continuing with the reading.

Read this aloud with children of any age. I used to be amazed when meeting older toddlers who could speak two or three languages, which was not uncommon in places where I have lived. But no longer. I have seen it enough to know that if parents are talking frequently or all day to their children, the children are learning. How else would toddlers come to understand multiple languages? If they can hear your voice, they are learning.

Start Late - How many of us first learned that "Ajax" was the name of a famous character in literature—not just a brand of scouring powder we used to scrub the sink—only after reading the *Iliad* for the first time, as late as in high school or college? For many of us who attended school after the 1940s, our education was sadly lacking, and mastery of a subject may be out of reach. But then again, maybe not. Get started here with this book. If you would like ideas about next steps and additional reading, visit www.findingour-words.com to learn about other Mount Titano Media books, and for articles about self-directed education, homeschooling (whether full-time or supplementing outside school), and leisure learning.

Make Vocabulary Cards and Use a Dictionary - When we read extraordinary works, we will encounter words which we may be able to understand in context but not define, words with subtle nuances we do not catch, and words we have never seen. To build our vocabulary, we need to read not in dread of the "hard" words, but looking forward with hope to discovering them.

For this subject, the English word "vocabulary" is lack-luster. I prefer the German word for vocabulary: Wortschatz. Wort means "word" and Schatz means "treasure"… word-treasure. The pen is mightier than the sword, and words are a greater treasure than diamonds and pearls. Do not leave your treasure scattered among the pages—gather your words as you go and store them in your treasure chest.

We have kept vocabulary index card rings built from our readings from the time my child began to read, and for each word we looked up, we made a new card. We would write the word (using phonetic symbols to help with pronunciation), the part of speech, the definition, and the sentence in which we found it. Including the entire sentence has done more than just help us to remember the word. It has shown the word at the pinnacle of its career. It is exasperating and essentially a waste of time to use pre-made vocabulary card sets that usually cast strong and noble vocabulary words into the dungeon of absurd, illogical, and demeaning sentences. Adorn your own word-treasure cards with sentences from the greatest works of all time.

Ideas For Reading This Book

Skip Some: If the writing in any section of this book is out of reach for you, your student, or your child, do not let it slow you down. Skip it for now, and come back in a few months or a few years. But do come back to it.

Begin to Practice Elocution - Elocution was once a standard part of school curricula. It has not been so for the last hundred years or more, and we hear the results all around us. This book is not an elocution course, but a few tips can get us started. When having children read aloud, encourage them to incorporate a manner of expression appropriate to the text and dialogue. Encourage them to project their voices. A favorite word we have used in reading great works aloud is "stentorian." In the days before micro-phones and speakers, a stentorian voice was required if one wished to be heard.

Take Your Time - The works of Homer have been read for millennia, and individuals read them repeatedly through-out their lifetime. For some readers, these works are too rich to consume in large portions. Enjoy the amount that is satis-fying in one sitting, and come back for more later, and from now on. Some inspiration in this regard:

> *A professor*[1] *whose work I follow told of his father, who when lying in his hospital bed near the end of his life, had the works of Homer, Virgil, and other greats around him at all times (all in the original languages). A nurse told the professor:"You have got to make your father stop staying up late reading those books. It's going to kill him." The wise professor, filial son, replied: "Reading those books is what's keeping him alive."*

Struggle - Reading works from another era can some-times be challenging. But if you take your time and read in small doses, the struggle will never be a burden. It will be what author Tracy Lee Simmons describes elsewhere as

> *...an entrée to greatness...through a daily struggle with clear and constant examples of superior perception and utterance.*

Practice Leisure - Less than a century ago, and stretch-ing back to antiquity, "leisure" summoned scenes other than those one might imagine today: strolls through a forest,

[1] www.alexanderarguelles.com

riding through the countryside on horseback; or time at home with family or a gathering of friends, playing musical instruments and singing, or reading aloud from great works by fireside or in the garden.

Whatever the leisurely pursuit, the purpose was to restore, invigorate, and enrich one's life. The mood created by reading great works aloud together shifts us away from "doing homework" and into a reward that is anticipated with joy. For instance, I have created a ritual around reading aloud by doing so outside when possible and serving rose tea. Create your own rituals. Small touches added to a routine can transform the scene from one of drudgery to the high-light of one's day, to a beloved tradition, and to the making of multigenerational memories.

It is exhilarating to realize how much one can learn, and how much can quietly change within one's self and within one's family, simply by reading great stories, slowly, and making them one's own.

—Allison Ellis

— INTRODUCTION —

We live in a chaotic, levelling age when one can no longer, with calm assurance, distinguish the educated from the uneducated. And diplomas and degrees earned by schools and higher institutions, which once certified one's intellectual heft and mettle, tell us little to nothing. Today the vocabulary and syntax used by an Ivy Leaguer are unlikely to be conspicuously superior to that of a high school dropout, so inefficacious and flattening has standard schooling become. Yet not even school attendance has always served predictably as a prime indicator of a formed intelligence. There was a time when one's facility with words, with verbal expression serving both simple and sophisticated purposes, could identify with a high degree of confidence the educated man or woman, regardless of that person's academic background. The unschooled were not *ipso facto* the uneducated. And so it is in our own day, and perhaps increasingly so. The educated mind, it would seem, has become an ever more fugitive achievement.

This has not always been so. In the world of classical Greece, one could tell who was educated by the penetrating fact that he knew the poems of Homer, and more than a few people could recite much of them. The educated man knew Homer, and Homer was what he knew. He had taken it in with mother's milk. All else, however vital for a cultivated people, was scaffolding. Those two poems, *Iliad* and *Odyssey*, afforded and indeed enforced a common language, a common set of references; they were a kind of scripture for the Greek mind; they defined the Hellenic spirit—and, of course, what the Greeks knew the Romans came to know in equal measure. Without exaggeration, we can say that the intellectual and spiritual essence of Western civilization began with Homer and, for all we know, could end with an ignorance of him. But no matter the state of our culture, the Western mind remains Homer-haunted.

One droll line from the academy of footnoting scholars has it that the *Iliad* and *Odyssey* were not really written by Homer but by another man of the same name, a joke that underlines the mystery of just who it was who committed the Homeric poems to parchment or to some other serviceable surface so long ago. Was he one man? A committee? A woman? We do not really know. Our best guess for the date of composition, whoever scribed the words, is sometime around the 8th century B.C. More important for us to know, though, is that those two epic poems were born of recitation, of a rhapsode's chant around campfires. They were bardic, mesmeric incantations that sang of heroes and wars, sea journeys and battlefields, love and lust, justice and mercy, pride and sacrifice, life and death. The eternal predicament.

"War is the father of all," Heraclitus would pre-Socratically say two or three centuries later, but anybody who knew the Homeric stories didn't need to be told. The fact was manifest. War, arising as it does out of the darker synapses of human nature, cannot be eradicated, and those who claim it can are to be relegated to the ranks of the unwise. And yet, the civilized mind claims, war can be ennobled, no matter the cause, and that even brutality can be tamed and, ultimately, redeemed. The *Iliad* lends to posterity one long tale of how such redemption can begin to peer through the smoke and shine its rays over mountaintops. But as it is also a tale that educated people used to know, it comes equipped with object lessons for those with ears to hear—lessons on how to live, how to react, how to endure, how to die. Little wonder that it was known and cherished for so many centuries. Readers could see themselves peering out of its lines, which, by the by, is what makes it literature.

The *Iliad* is not just a story. It's a small universe. On the Achaean side, we find the intrepid Achilles, driven mad by anger; Agamemnon and Menelaus, chieftains whose honor has been offended by what was to their lights a rash act of abduction; Calchas the seer; Idomeneus of Crete, who has joined the fight; the self-sacrificing Antilochus; Odysseus, *polytropos*, the skilled warrior of many turns who will return in the next epic poem; and Patroclus, the boon companion of Achilles. On the Trojan side, we meet King Priam and Queen Hecuba; the brave Hector, son of Priam; Andromache, his wife; Cassandra, Hector's prophetess sister; Paris, his brother who abducted Helen, wife of Menelaus; and Aeneas, who, like Odysseus, will return in a later epic to found another city-state and people to the west. All of these and many others come together to wage war on the "ringing plains of windy Troy," a war that none of them—save one—started but who now must all fight and suffer, both on the battlefield and on the home front, to the bitter end. Looming over all, of course, the gods of Olympus, who push and pull with their own loyalties and jealousies, using the human actors below as playthings. And we are left, nearly three millennia later, to wonder about the mysteries of Fate and Destiny, as well as the wages of Pride and Anger. The closer we look, the better we see ourselves.

But why read the book in your hands instead of turning headlong to a full translation of what Homer wrote? For this book is not the poem, however faithfully or loosely translated, but it is the *story*—and it is with story that our curiosity begins and seeks satisfaction. Yet while this is not a replacement for the full poem, it's a fine and thoroughgoing preparation for it. It tells the tale. It introduces the *dramatis personae*. It reveals the plot. Anybody of any age who reads these pages will have no trouble when meeting the poem itself in all its splendor. After reading this book, one is well-armored for the rigors and scattered ambiguities of any translation and—*deo volente*—for tackling the original in Homeric Greek someday.

Which is what its author, the formidable Alfred John Church (1829-1912), classical scholar, headmaster, and professor of Latin at University College, London, sought to do: to prepare younger readers for the intoxicating pleasures of the deep diving in bracing waters to come in their reading lives. He was an evangelist of sorts. Church sought above all to put the classics of ancient Greece and Rome within reach of the young who were still, and might remain, Greek-less and Latin-less—an office later performed just as ably and brilliantly by Edith Hamilton. Church was a man whose scholastic attainments did not cancel an overriding drive to serve a wider public. Unfortunately, his work has been largely ignored over the last century as unworthy of serious notice, which only shows how culpably dismissive self-absorbed, myopic minds can be.

It is often said that "poetry is what gets lost in translation". True enough. But only the poetry, the music, is lost—not the story, the drama, the reason the novice reader approaches a book or poem to begin with. And that first ingredient of satisfaction the reader can and will get here and so will be much better primed for the greater delights to come. Here we find all 15,693 lines of dactylic hexameter boiled down to their essence. The grace notes may be gone, those thunderous syllabic echoes of hammered language, but the story remains, ever present, like the Chinese jar in T.S. Eliot "moving perpetually in its stillness."

Yet no matter how much Homer stood as the beginning and basis of education in the West, there was no reason not to have a bit of fun with him, and his work could be put to lighter uses. For parody too seems part of human instinct. Perhaps as early as the 5th century B.C.—though somewhat more likely in the early years of the Roman Empire—a fancifully comic send-off on the *Iliad*, of unknown authorship, appeared to the felicity of all who knew the story, which was pretty much everybody. Anticipating Orwell's *Animal Farm* by a couple thousand years, the *Batrachomyomachia*, or "The Battle of the Frogs and Mice," imagined a protracted struggle amongst animals in which the gods intervened at will. The work's popularity in the Hellenistic and Roman ages has been attested by Plutarch, but as the West maintained a fundamentally classical curriculum well into the Middle Ages and beyond, it too has been a source of delectation in later centuries, being translated several times. Provided here are three renderings into English by Hugh G. Evelyn-White (1914), the poet William Cowper (1791), and the estimable George Chapman (1624). Together they present a rousing miscellany of lines that, according to the period taste of the English reader, make fine fodder for memorization and recitation.

We see the *Iliad* all around us. It's there every time we hear of wars or the rumors of wars. Its furtive lessons and pressing admonitions to curb human excesses hang over our heads, brooding, every time we see a new conflagration flare up anywhere in the world. And as war will always be with us, we might as well drink from the fountain and learn those lessons directly. This is our inheritance. We should claim it, and we claim it by reading.

—Tracy Lee Simmons

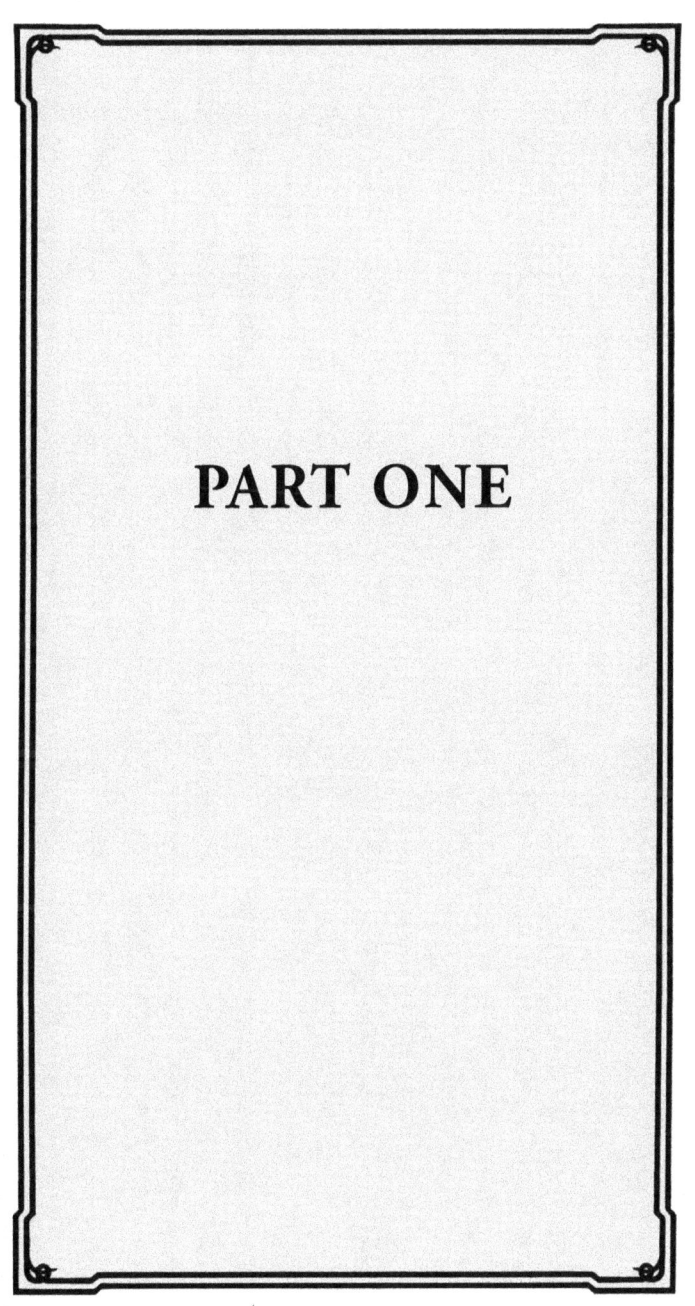

PART ONE

THE STORY OF THE ILIAD

CHAPTER I

OF HOW THE WAR WITH TROY BEGAN

Once upon a time there was a certain King of Sparta who had a most beautiful daughter, Helen by name. There was not a prince in Greece but wished to marry her. The King said to them: "Now you must all swear that you will be good friends with the man whom my daughter shall choose for her husband, and that if anyone is wicked enough to steal her away from him, you will help him to get her back." And this they did. Then the Fair Helen chose a prince whose name was Menelaus, brother of Agamemnon, who reigned in Mycenae, and was the chief of all the Kings of Greece. After a while Helen's father died, and her husband became King of Sparta. The two lived happily together till there came to Sparta a young prince, Paris by name, who was son of Priam, King of Troy. This Paris car-

ried off the Fair Helen, and with her much gold and many
precious stones.

Menelaus and his brother Agamemnon sent to the
princes of Greece and said, "Now you must keep your oath,
and help us to get back the Fair Helen."

So they all came to a place called Aulis, with many ships
and men. Others also who had not taken the oath came with
them. The greatest of these chiefs were these:

Diomed, son of Tydeus; Ajax the Greater and Ajax the
Less, and Teucer the Archer, who was brother of Ajax the
Greater.

Nestor, who was the oldest man in the world.

The wise Ulysses.

Achilles, who was the bravest and strongest of all the
Greeks, and with him his dear friend Patroclus.

For nine years the Greeks besieged the city of Troy, but
they could not break through the walls; and as they had been
away from their homes for all this time, they came to be in
great want of food and clothes and other things. So they left
part of the army to watch the city, and with part they went
about and spoiled other cities. Thus came about the great
quarrel of which I am now going to tell.

CHAPTER II

THE QUARREL

The Greeks took the city of Chryse and divided the spoils among the chiefs, and to Agamemnon they gave a girl named Chryseis, who was the daughter of the priest of Apollo, the god who was worshipped in the city. Then the priest came bringing much gold, with which he wished to buy back his daughter.

First of all he went to Agamemnon and his brother, and then to the other chiefs, and begged them to take the gold and give him back the girl. "So," he said, "may the gods help you to take the city of Troy, and bring you back safe to your homes."

All the other chiefs were willing, but Agamemnon cried, "Away with you, old man. Do not linger here now, and do not come again, or it will be the worse for you, though you are a priest. As for your daughter, I will carry her back with me when I have taken Troy."

So the old man went out in great fear and trouble, and he prayed to Apollo to help him. And Apollo heard him. Very angry was the god that his priest should suffer such things, and he came down from his palace on the top of the mountain Olympus. He came as night comes across the sky, and his arrows rattled terribly as he went. Then he began to shoot, and his arrows carried death, first to the dogs and the mules, and then to the men. For nine days the people died, and on the tenth day Achilles called an assembly.

When the Greeks were gathered together he stood up in the middle and said: "Surely it would be better to go home than to stay here and die. Many are slain in battle, and still more are slain by the plague. Let us ask the prophets why it is that Apollo is angry with us."

Then Calchas the prophet stood up: "You wish to know why Apollo is angry. I will tell you, but first you must promise to stand by me, for King Agamemnon will be angry when he hears what I shall say."

"Say on," cried Achilles; "no man shall harm you while I live, no, not Agamemnon himself."

Then Calchas said: "Apollo is angry because, when his priest came to buy back his daughter, Agamemnon would not listen to him. Now you must send back the girl, taking no money for her, and with her a hundred beasts as a sacrifice."

Then King Agamemnon stood up in a rage and cried: "You always prophesy evil, ill prophet that you are. The girl I

ATHENE SUPPRESSING THE FURY OF ACHILLES

will send back, for I would not have the people die, but I will not go without my share of the spoil."

"You think too much of gain, King Agamemnon," said Achilles. "Surely you would not take from any man that which has been given him. Wait till Troy has been conquered, and then we will make up to you what you have lost three times over."

"Do not try to cheat me in this way," answered Agamemnon. "My share I will have at once. If the Greeks will give it to me, well and good but if not, then I will take it from one of the chiefs, from you, Achilles, or from Ajax, or from Ulysses. But now let us see about the sending back of the girl."

Then Achilles was altogether carried away with rage and said: "Never was there a king so shameless and so greedy of gain. The Trojans never did harm to me or mine. I have been fighting against them for your sake and your brother's. And you sit in your tent at ease, but when the spoil is divided, then you have the lion's share. And now you will take the little that was given me. I will not stay here to be shamed and robbed. I will go home."

"Go," said Agamemnon, "and take your people with you. I have other chiefs as good as you, and ready to honour me, as you are not. But mark this: the girl Briseis, who was given to you as your share of the spoil, I will take, if I have to come and fetch her myself. For you must learn that I am master here."

Achilles was mad with anger to hear this, and said to himself, "Now I will slay this villain where he sits," and he half drew his sword from its scabbard. But at that instant the goddess Athene stood behind him and seized him by his long yellow hair. And when he turned to see who had done this, he perceived the goddess—but no one else in the assembly could see her—and said: "Are you come to see this villain die?"

"Nay," she answered, "I am come to stay your rage. Queen Hera and I love you both. Draw not your sword, but say what you will. Some day he will pay you back three times and four times for all the wrong that he shall do."

Achilles answered: "I will do as you bid for he who hears the gods is heard by them." So he thrust back his sword into the scabbard, and Athene went back to Olympus. Then he turned to Agamemnon and cried: "Drunkard with the eyes of a dog and the heart of a deer, hear what I tell you now. See this sceptre that I have in my hand. Once it was the branch of a tree, now a king carries it in his hand. As surely as it will never more shoot forth in leaves, so surely will the Greeks one day miss Achilles. And you, when you see your people falling by the swords of the Trojans, will be sorry that you have done this wrong to the bravest man in your army." And he dashed the sceptre on the ground and sat down.

Then the old man Nestor stood up and would have made peace between the two. "Listen to me," he said. "Great chiefs of old, with whom no one now alive would dare to fight, were used to listen to me. You, King Agamemnon, do not take away from the brave Achilles the gift that the Greeks gave him and you, Achilles, pay due respect to him who is the King of Kings in Greece."

So spoke Nestor, but he spoke in vain, for Agamemnon answered: "Peace is good; but this fellow would lord it over all. The gods have made him a great warrior, but they have not given him leave to set himself up above law and order. He must learn that there is one here better than he."

And Achilles cried: "You better than me! I were a slave and a coward if I owned it. What the Greeks gave me, let them take away if they will. But mark this: if you lay your hands on anything that is my own, that hour you die."

Then the assembly was broken up. After a while Agamemnon said to the heralds: "Go now to the tent of Achilles, and fetch thence the girl Briseis. And if he will not let her go, say that I will come with others to fetch her, and that it will be the worse for him."

So the heralds went, but it was much against their will that they did this errand. And when they came to that part of the camp where Achilles and his people were, they found him sitting between his tent and his ship. And they stood in great fear and shame. But when he saw them he spoke kind words to them, for all that his heart was full of rage. "Draw near, heralds. 'Tis no fault of yours that you are come on such an errand." Then he turned to Patroclus and said: "Fetch Briseis from her tent and give her to the heralds. Let them be witnesses of this evil deed, that they may remember it in the day when he shall need my help and shall not have it."

So Patroclus brought out the girl and gave her to the heralds. And she went with them, much against her will, and often looking back. And when she was gone, Achilles left his companions and sat upon the seashore, weeping aloud and stretching out his hands to his mother Thetis, the daughter of the sea. She heard his voice where she sat in the depths by the side of her father, and rose from the sea, as a cloud rises, and came to him where he sat weeping, shaking him with her hand, and calling him by his name.

"Why do you weep, my son?" she said.

And he told her what had been done. And when he had finished the story, he said: "Now go to Olympus, to the palace of Zeus. You helped him once in the old time, when the other gods would have put him in chains, fetching the great giant with the hundred hands to sit by his side, so that no one dared to touch him. Remind him of these things, and ask him to help the Trojans, and to make the Greeks flee before them, so that Agamemnon may learn how foolish he has been."

His mother said: "Surely, my son, your lot is very hard. Your life must be short, and it should be happy; but, as it seems to me, it is both short and sad. Truly I will go to Zeus, but not now; for he is gone with the other gods to a Twelve Days' feast. But when he comes back, then I will go to him and persuade him. Meanwhile do you sit still, and do not go forth to battle."

Meanwhile Ulysses was taking back the priest's daughter to her father. Very glad was he to see her again, and he prayed to his god that the plague among the Greeks might cease, and so it happened. But Achilles sat in his tent and fretted, for there was nothing that he liked so much as the cry of the battle.

CHAPTER III

WHAT THETIS DID FOR HER SON

When the twelve days of feasting were over, Thetis rose out of the sea and went her way to Olympus. There she found Zeus sitting alone on the highest peak of the mountain. She knelt down before him, and her left hand she laid upon his knees, and with her right she caught hold of his beard. Then she made this prayer to him:—

"O father Zeus, if I have ever helped thee at all, now give me what I ask, namely, that my son Achilles may have honour done to him. Agamemnon has shamed him, taking away the gift that the Greeks gave him. Do thou, therefore, make the Trojans prevail for a while in battle, so that the Greeks may find that they cannot do without him. So shall my son have honour."

For a long time Zeus sat saying nothing, for he knew that great trouble would come out of this thing. But Thetis still held him fast by the knees and by the beard and she spoke again, saying: "Promise me this thing, and make your promise sure by nodding your head; or, else, say outright that you will not do it. Then I shall know that you despise me."

Zeus answered: "This is a hard thing that you ask. You will make a dreadful quarrel between me and the Lady Hera, my wife, and she will say many bitter words to me. Even now she tells me that I favour the Trojans too much. Go, then, as quickly as you can, that she may not know that you have been here, and I will think how I may best do what you ask. And see, I will make my promise sure with a nod, for when I nod my head, then the thing may not be repented of or undone."

So he nodded his head, and all Olympus was shaken.

Then Thetis went away, and dived down into the sea. And Zeus went to his palace, and when he came in at the door, all the gods rose up in their places, and stood till he sat down on his throne. But Hera knew that Thetis had been with him, and she was very angry, and spoke bitter words: "Who has been with you, O lover of plots? When I am not here, then you take a pleasure in hiding what you do, and in keeping things from me."

Zeus answered: "O Hera, do not think to know all my thoughts; that is too hard for you, even though you are my wife. That which it is right for you to know, I will tell you before I tell it to any other god, but there are matters which I keep to myself. Do not seek to know these."

But Hera was even more angry than before. "What say you?" she cried. "I do not pry into your affairs. Settle them as you will. But this I know, that Thetis with the silver feet has been with you, and I greatly fear that she has had her way. At dawn of day I saw her kneeling before you; yes, and you nodded your head. I am sure that you have promised her that Achilles should have honour. Ah me! many of the Greeks will die for this."

Then Zeus answered: "Truly there is nothing that you do not find out, witch that you are. But, if it be as you say, then know that such is my will. Do you sit still and obey. All the gods in Olympus cannot save you, if once I lay my hands upon you."

Hera sat still and said nothing, for she was very much afraid. Then her son, the god who made arms and armour and cups and other things out of silver and gold and copper, said to her:

"It would be a great pity if you and the Father of the gods should quarrel on account of a man. Make peace with him, and do not make him angry again. It would be a great grief to me if I were to see you beaten before my eyes; for, indeed, I could not help you. Once before when I tried to come between him and you, he took me by the foot and threw me out of the door of heaven. All day I fell, and at evening I lighted in the island of Lemnos."

Then he thought how he might turn the thoughts of the company to something else. There was a very beautiful boy who used to carry the wine round. The god, who was a cripple, took his place, and mixed the cup, and hobbled round with it, puffing for breath as he went, and all the gods fell into great fits of laughter when they saw him.

So the feast went on, and Apollo and the Muses sang, and no one thought any more about the quarrel.

But while all the other gods were sleeping, Zeus remained awake, thinking how he might do what Thetis had asked of him for her son. The best thing seemed to be to deceive Agamemnon, and make him think that he could take the city of Troy without the help of Achilles. So he called a Dream, and said to it: "Go, Dream, to the tent of Agamemnon, and tell him that if he will lead his army to battle, he will take the city of Troy."

So the Dream went, and it took the shape of Nestor, whom the King thought to be the wisest of the Greeks, and stood by his bedside and said: "Why do you waste your time in sleep? Arm the Greeks, and lead them out to battle, for you will take the city of Troy."

And the King believed that this false dream was true.

CHAPTER IV

THE DUEL OF PARIS AND MENELAUS

On the day after the False Dream had come to him, Agamemnon called all his army to go out to battle. All the chiefs were glad to fight, for they thought that at last the long war was coming to an end. Only Achilles and his people stopped behind. And the Trojans, on the other hand, set their army in order.

Before they began to fight, Paris, who had been the cause of all the trouble, came out in front of the line. He had a panther's skin over his shoulders, and a bow and a quiver slung upon his back, for he was a great archer; by his side there hung a sword, and in each hand he carried a spear. He cried aloud to the Greeks: "Send out the strongest and bravest man you have to fight with me."

When King Menelaus heard this, he said to himself: "Now this is my enemy; I will fight with him, and no one else."

So he jumped down from his chariot, and ran out in front of the line of Greeks. But when Paris saw him he was very much afraid, and turned his back and ran behind the line of the Trojans.

Now the best and bravest of the Trojans was a certain Hector. He was one of the sons of King Priam, and if it had not been for him the city would have been taken long before. When he saw Paris run away he was very angry, and said: "O Paris, you are good to look at, but you are worth nothing. And the Greeks think that you are the bravest man we have! You were brave enough to go across the sea to steal the Fair Helen from her husband, and now when he comes out to fight with you, you run away. The Trojans ought to have stoned you to death long ago."

Paris answered: "You speak the truth, great Hector; I am, indeed, greatly to be blamed. As for you, you care for nothing but battles, and your heart is made of iron. But now listen to me: set Menelaus and me to fight, man to man, and let him that conquers have the Fair Helen and all her possessions. If he kills me, let him take her and depart; but if I kill him, then she shall stay here. So, whatever may happen, you will dwell in peace."

Hector was very glad to hear his brother Paris speak in this way. And he went along the line of the Trojans, holding his spear in the middle. This he did to show that he was not meaning to fight, and to keep his men in their places that they should not begin the battle. At first the Greeks made ready spears and stones to throw at him, but Agamemnon cried out: "Hold your hands; great Hector has something to say."

Then everyone stood still and listened. And Hector said: "Hear, Trojans and Greeks, what Paris says, Paris, who is the cause of this quarrel between us. 'Let Menelaus and me fight together. Everyone else, whether he is Greek or Trojan, shall lay his arms upon the ground, and look on while we two fight together. For the Fair Helen and her riches we will fight, and the rest will cease from war and be good friends forever.'"

When Hector had spoken, King Menelaus stood up and said: "Listen to me, for this is my affair. It is well that the Greeks and Trojans should be at peace, for there is no quarrel between them. Let me and Paris fight together, and let him of us two be slain whose fate it is to die. And now let us make a sacrifice to the gods, and swear a great oath over it that we will keep to our agreement. Only let King Priam himself come and offer the sacrifice and take the oath, for he is more to be trusted than the young men his sons."

So spoke Menelaus; and both the armies were glad, for they were tired of the war.

Then Hector sent a messenger to Troy to fetch King Priam, and to bring sheep for the sacrifice. And while the herald was on his way, one of the gods put it into the heart of the Fair Helen as she sat in her hall to go out to the wall and see the army of the Greeks. So she went, leaving the needlework with which she was busy, a great piece of embroidery, on which the battles between the Greeks and the Trojans were worked.

Now King Priam sat on the wall, and with him were the other princes of the city, old men who could no longer fight, but could take counsel and make beautiful speeches. They saw the Fair Helen as she came, and one of them said to another: "See how beautiful she is! And yet it would be better that she should go back to her own country, than that she should stop here and bring a curse upon us and our children."

But Priam called to her and said: "Come hither, my daughter, and see your friends and kinsmen in yonder army, and tell us about them. Who is that warrior there, so fair and strong? There are others who are even a head taller than he is, but there is no one who is so like a king."

"That," said Helen, "is Agamemnon, a brave soldier and a wise king, and my brother- in-law in the old days."

And King Priam cried: "Happy Agamemnon, to rule over so many brave men as I see in yonder army! But tell me who is that warrior there, who is walking through the ranks of his men, and making them stand in good order? He is not so tall as Agamemnon, but he is broader in the shoulders."

"That," said Helen, "is Ulysses of Ithaca, who is wiser than all other men, and gives better advice."

"You speak truly, fair lady," said one of the old men, Antenor by name. "Well do I remember Ulysses when he came with Menelaus on an embassy. They were guests in my house, and I knew them well. And when there was an assembly of the Trojans to hear them speak on the business for which they came, I remember how they looked. When they were standing, Menelaus was the taller; but when they sat down, then Ulysses was the nobler of the two to look at. And when they spoke, Menelaus said but a few words, and said them wisely and well; and Ulysses—at first you might have taken him to be a fool, so stiffly did he hold his staff, and so awkward did he seem, with his eyes cast down upon the ground, but when he began to speak, how grand was his voice and how his words poured out, thick as the falling snow! There never was a speaker such as he, and we thought no more about his looks."

Then King Priam asked again: "Who is that mighty hero, so big and strong, taller than all the rest by his head and shoulders?"

"That," said Helen, "is Ajax, a tower of strength to the Greeks. And other chiefs I see whom I know and could name. But my own dear brothers, Castor, tamer of horses, and Pollux, the mighty boxer, I see not. Is it that they are ashamed to come on account of me?"

So she spoke, not knowing that they were dead.

And now came the messenger to tell King Priam that the armies wanted him. So he went and Antenor with him, and they took the sheep for sacrifice. Then King Priam, on behalf of the Trojans, and King Agamemnon, on behalf of the Greeks, offered sacrifice, and made an agreement, confirming it with an oath, that Menelaus and Paris should fight together, and that Fair Helen with her treasure should belong to him who should prevail.

When this was done, King Priam said: "I will go back to Troy, for I could not bear to see my dear son fighting with Menelaus." So he climbed into the chariot, and Antenor took the reins and they went back to Troy.

Then Hector for the Trojans, and Ulysses for the Greeks, marked out a space for the fight, and Hector put two pebbles into a helmet, one for Paris and one for Menelaus. These he shook, looking away as he did so, for it was agreed that the man whose pebble should first fly out of the helmet, should be the first to cast his spear at the other. And this might be much to his gain, for the spear, being well thrown, might kill his adversary or wound him to death, and he himself would not come into danger. And it so happened that the pebble of Paris first flew out. Then the two warriors armed themselves, and came into the space that had been marked out, and stood facing each other. Very fierce were their eyes, so that it could be seen how they hated each other. First Paris threw his spear. It hit the shield of Menelaus, but did not pierce it, for the point was bent back. Then Menelaus threw his spear; but first he prayed: "Grant, Father Zeus, that I may have vengeance on Paris, who has done me this great wrong!" And the spear went right through the shield, and through the armour that Paris wore upon his body, and through the tunic that was under the armour. But Paris shrank away, so that the spear did not wound him.

Then Menelaus drew his sword, and struck the helmet of Paris on the top with a great blow, but the sword was broken into four pieces. Then he rushed upon Paris and caught him by the helmet, and dragged him towards the army of the Greeks; neither could Paris help himself, for the strap of the helmet choked him. Then, indeed, would Paris have been taken prisoner and killed, but that the goddess Aphrodite helped him, for he was her favourite. She loosed the strap under his chin, and the helmet came off in the hand of Menelaus. The King threw it among the Greeks, and, taking another spear in his hand, ran furiously at Paris. But the goddess covered him with a mist, and so snatched him away, and set him down in his own house at Troy. Everywhere did Menelaus look for him, but he could not find him. It was no one of the Trojans that hid him, for they all hated him as death.

Then said King Agamemnon in a loud voice: "Now must you Trojans keep the covenant that you have made with an oath. You must give back the Fair Helen and her treasures, and we will take her and leave you in peace."

CHAPTER V

HOW THE OATH WAS BROKEN

ow, if the Trojans had kept the promise which they had made, confirming it with an oath, it would have been well with them. But it was not to be. And this is how it came to pass that the oath was broken and the promise was not kept.

Among the chiefs who came from the countries round about to help King Priam and the Trojans there was a certain Pandarus, son of the King of Lycia. He was a great archer, and could shoot an arrow as far and with as good an aim as any man in the army. To this Pandarus, as he stood waiting for what should next happen, there came a youth, a son of King Priam. Such, indeed, he seemed to be, but in truth the goddess Athene had taken his shape, for she and, as has been before said, the goddess Hera hated the city of Troy, and desired to bring it to ruin.

The false Trojan came up to Pandarus, as he stood among his men, and said to him: "Prince of Lycia, dare you shoot an arrow at Menelaus? Truly the Trojans would love you well, and Paris best of all, if they could see Menelaus killed with an arrow from your bow. Shoot at him as he stands, not thinking of any danger, but first vow to sacrifice a hundred beasts to Zeus, so soon as you shall get back to your own country."

Pandarus had a bow made out of the horns of a wild goat which he had killed. It was four feet long from end to end, and on each end there was a tip of gold on which the bow-string was fixed. While he was stringing his bow, his men stood round and hid him and when he had strung it, he took an arrow from his quiver, and laid it on the string, and drew back the string till it touched his breast, and then let the arrow fly. But though none of the Greeks saw what Pandarus was doing, Athene saw it, and she flew to where Menelaus stood, and kept the arrow from doing him a deadly hurt. She would not ward it off altogether, for she knew that the Greeks would be angry to see the King whom they loved so treacherously wounded, and would have no peace with the Trojans. So she guided it to where there was a space between the belt and the breastplate. There it struck the King, passing through the edge of the belt and through the garment that was under the belt and piercing the skin and the red blood gushed out, and dyed the thighs and the legs and the ankles of the King, as a woman dyes a piece of white ivory to make an ornament for a king's warhorse.

Now Agamemnon was standing near, and when he saw the blood gush out he cried: "Oh, my brother, it was a foolish thing that I did, when I made a covenant with the Trojans, for they are wicked men and break their oaths. I know that they who do such things will suffer for them. Sooner or later the man who breaks his oath will perish miserably. Nevertheless, it will be a great shame and sorrow if you, my brother, should be killed in this way. For the Greeks will go to their homes, saying: 'Why should we fight any more for Menelaus, seeing that he is dead?' And the Fair Helen for whom we have been fighting these many years will be left behind; and one of these false Trojans will say when he sees the tomb of Menelaus: 'Surely the great Agamemnon has not got that for which he came. For he brought a great army to destroy the city of Troy, but Troy still stands, and he and his army have gone back: only he has left his brother behind him.'"

But Menelaus said: "Do not trouble yourself, my brother, for the wound is not deep. See, here is the barb of the arrow."

Then King Agamemnon commanded that they should fetch Machaon, the great physician. So Machaon came, and drew the arrow out of the wound, and wiped away the blood, and put healing drugs upon the place, which took away all the pain.

After this King Agamemnon went through the army to see that it was ready for battle. When he found anyone bestirring himself, putting his men in order, and doing such things as it was his duty to do, him he praised; and if he saw any one idle and slow to move, him he rebuked. When all were ready, then the host went forward. In silence it went; but the Trojans, on the other hand, were as noisy as a flock of sheep, which bleats when they hear the voice of the lambs.

CHAPTER VI

THE GREAT DEEDS OF DIOMED

Many great deeds were done that day, and many chiefs showed themselves to be valiant men, but the greatest deeds were done by Diomed, and of all the chiefs there was not one who could be matched with him. No one could tell, so fierce was he, and so swiftly did he charge, in which host he was fighting, whether with the Greeks or with the sons of Troy. After a while the great archer Pandarus aimed an arrow at him, and hit him on the right shoulder. And when Pandarus saw that he had hit him, for the blood started out from the wound, he cried out in great joy: "On, men of Troy; I have wounded the bravest of the Greeks. He will soon either fall dead in his chariot, or grow so weak that he can fight no longer."

But Diomed was not to be conquered in this fashion. He leapt down from his chariot, and said to the man who drove the horses: "Come and draw this arrow out of the wound."

And this the driver did, and when Diomed saw the blood spurt out from the wound he prayed to the goddess Athene: "O goddess, stand by me, as you did always stand by my father. And as for the man who has wounded me, let him come within a spear's cast of me, and he will never boast again."

And Athene heard his prayer, and came and stood beside him, and took away the pain from his wound, and put new strength into his hands and feet. "Be bold, O Diomed, and fight against the men of Troy. As I stood by your father, so will I stand by you."

Then Diomed fought even more fiercely than before, just as a lion which a shepherd has wounded a little when he leaps into the fold grows yet more savage, so it was with Diomed. And as he went to and fro through the battle, slaying all whom he met, Tineas, who was the bravest of the Trojans after Hector, thought how he might best be stopped. So he passed through the army till he came to where Pandarus the archer stood.

To him he said: "Where are your bow and arrows? Do you see this man how he is dealing death wherever he goes? Shoot an arrow at him; but first make your prayers to Zeus that you may not shoot in vain."

Pandarus answered: "This man is Diomed. I know his shield and his helmet; the horses too are his. Some god, I am sure, stands by him and defends him. Only just now I sent an arrow at him, yes, and hit him in the shoulder. I thought that I had wounded him to the death, for I saw the blood spurt out; but I have not hurt him at all. And now I do not know what I can do, for I have no chariot here. Eleven chariots I have at home, and my father would have had me bring one of them with me. But I would not, for I was afraid that the horses would not have provender[1] enough, being shut up in the city of Troy. So I came without a chariot, trusting in my bow, and lo! it has failed me these two times. Two of the chiefs I have hit, first Menelaus and then this Diomed. Yes, I hit them, and I saw the red blood flow, but I have not harmed them. Surely if ever I get back safe to my home, I will break this useless bow."

---

[1] Editor's Note on the word "provender":

"Provender" a word not commonly used since the late 19th century, meaning "feed for domestic animals." From Latin "praebenda"—things to be supplied; to Middle English from Old French: "provendre."

Words have their own history, and the study of the history of words and how meaning has changed is called "etymology." Consider what the history of the word "provender" might reveal about world history. If you guessed that Latin made its way around continental Europe with the Roman Empire, and then found its way into Middle and then Present-Day English, in great part due to the Norman Conquest of 1066—you are correct.

Now consider why the use of the word "provender" essentially disappeared in modern discourse. Does it reveal anything about Present-Day English and our way of life?

A word of caution: If you do much more of this, it can become a habit, and you will be well on your way to becoming an "**etymologist**." That ending "-ologist" can be found in many words. What language does the suffix "-ologist" come from, you ask? It is from the Greek and means "someone who is an expert or studies in the field indicated in the root word; and in this example, the root word "etym" comes from the Greek word "etymos," meaning "true." So now you have learned the meaning and etymology of "provender" and the etymology of the word "etymology."

Last but not least, if you didn't already, you now know that even if we have never studied Greek and Latin, we are using them every time we speak! Now back to Pandarus and Diomed in Ancient Troy...

Then Aeneas said to him: "Nay, my friend, do not talk in this way. If you have no chariot, then come in mine, and see what horses we have in Troy. If Diomed should be too strong for us, still they will carry us safely back to Troy. Take the reins and the whip, and I will fight; or, if you would rather, do you fight and I will drive."

Pandarus said: "It is best that the horses should have the driver whom they know. If we should have to flee, they might stand still or turn aside, missing their master's voice."

Now Diomed was on foot, for he had not gone back to his chariot, and his charioteer was by his side. And the man said to him: "Look there; two mighty warriors, Pandarus and Aeneas, are coming against us. It would be well for us to go back to the chariot, that we may fight with them on equal terms."

But Diomed answered: "Do not talk of going back. I am not one of those who go back. As for my chariot, I do not want it. As I am, I will go against these men. Both of them, surely, shall not go back, even if one should escape. And if I slay them, then do you climb into the chariot and drive it away. There are no horses in the world as good as these, for they are of the breed which Zeus himself gave to King Tros."

While he was speaking the two Trojan chiefs came near, and Pandarus cast his spear at Diomed. It pierced the shield and also the belt, so strongly was it thrown, but it went no further. But Pandarus cried: "Aha! you are hit in the loin. This wound will stay you from fighting."

"Not so," said Diomed, "you have not wounded me at all. But now see what I will send."

DIOMED CASTING HIS SPEAR AGAINST ARES

And he threw his spear, nor did he throw in vain. The man fell from his chariot, and the armour clashed loudly upon him. But Aeneas would not leave his comrade. He leapt from the chariot, and stood with shield and spear over the body, as a lion stands over the carcass of some beast which it has killed. Now Diomed had no spear in his hand, neither could he draw out from the dead body that which he had thrown.

Therefore he stooped and took up from the ground a big stone so big was it that two men such as men are now could scarcely lift it up and threw it at Aeneas. On the hip it struck him and crushed the bone, and the hero fell upon his knees, and clutched at the ground with his hands, and everything grew dark before his eyes. Thus had he died, but for his mother, the goddess Aphrodite. She caught him up in her arms, and threw her veil over him to hide him. But Diomed did not like that he should escape, and he rushed with his spear at the goddess and wounded her in the arm, and the blood gushed out such blood as flows in the veins of gods, who eat not the food nor drink the drink of men. She dropped her son with a loud shriek and fled up into the sky.

And the bold Diomed called after her: "You should not join in the battle, daughter of Zeus. You have to do not with men but with women."

But Apollo caught up Aeneas when his mother dropped him. Even then Diomed was loath to let him escape, for he was bent on killing him and stripping him of his arms. Three times did he spring forward, and three times did Apollo put back his shining shield.

And when he came to the fourth time, Apollo called out to him in an awful voice: "Beware, Diomed, do not think to fight with gods."

Then Diomed fell back, for he was afraid. But Apollo carried Aeneas to the citadel of Troy, and there his mother Latona and his sister Artemis healed the hero of his wounds. But he left an image of the hero in the midst of the battle, and over him the Greeks and the Trojans fought, as if it had been the real Aeneas.

CHAPTER VII

CONCERNING OTHER VALIANT DEEDS

Now among the chiefs who came to help King Priam and the Trojans there was a certain Sarpedon, who was Prince of Lycia, and with him there was one Glaucus who was his cousin.

When Sarpedon saw how Diomed was laying waste the army of the Trojans, and that no man was willing or able to stand up against him, he said to Hector: "Where are your boasts, O Hector? You used to say that you could keep the city of Troy safe, without your people, and without us, who have come to help you. Yes, you and your brothers and your brothers-in-law would be enough, you said but now I look about me, and I cannot see one of them. They all go and hide themselves, as dogs before a lion. It is we who keep up the battle. Look at me; I have come far to help you, even from the land of Lycia, where I have left wife and child and wealth. Nor do I shrink back from the fight, but you also should do your part."

These words stung Hector to the heart. He jumped down from his chariot, and went through the army, telling the men to be brave. And Ares brought back Aeneas with his wound healed, and he himself went back with Hector, in the shape of a man. And even the brave Diomed, when he saw him, and knew that he was a god, held back a little, saying to his companions: "See, Hector is coming, and Ares is with him, in the shape of a man. Let us give way a little, for we must not fight with gods; but we will still keep our faces to the enemy."

Just then a great Greek warrior, who was one of the sons of Hercules, the strongest of men, was killed by Sarpedon the Lycian. This man cried out to Sarpedon: "What are you doing here? You are foolish to fight with men who are better than you are. Men say that you are a son of Zeus, but the sons of Zeus are braver and stronger than you. Are you as good as my father Hercules? Have you not heard how he came to this city of Troy, and broke down the walls, and spoiled the houses, because the King of Troy cheated him of his pay? For my father saved the King's daughter from a great monster of the sea, and the King promised him a team of horses, but did not keep his promise. And you have come to help the Trojans, so they say; small help will you be to them, when I have killed you."

Sarpedon answered: "It is true that your father broke down the walls of Troy, and spoiled the houses the King of the city had cheated him and he was rightly punished for it. But you shall not do what he did no, for I shall kill you first."

Then the two warriors threw their spears. At the same moment they threw them, and both of them hit the mark. The spear of Sarpedon went right through the neck of the Greek, so that he fell down dead and the spear of the Greek hit Sarpedon on the thigh of the left leg, and went through it close to the bone. It went very near to killing him; but it was not his fate to die that day. So his men carried him out of the battle, with the spear sticking in the wound, for no one thought of drawing it out, so great was their hurry. As they were carrying him along, Hector passed by, and he cried out: "O Hector, do not let the Greeks take me! Let me, at least, die in your city. I shall not go back nor shall I see again my wife and my child."

But Hector did not heed him, so eager was he to fight. So the men carried him to the great oak tree, and laid him down in the shade of it, and one of them drew the spear out of the wound. When it was drawn out he fainted, but the cool north wind blew on him and refreshed him, and he breathed again.

At this time the Greeks were being driven back; many were killed and many were wounded. For Hector, with Ares by his side, was so fierce and strong that no one dared to stand up against him. When the two goddesses, Hera and Athene, who loved the Greeks, saw this, they said to Zeus: "Father, do you see how furiously Ares is raging in the battle, driving the Greeks before him? May we stop him before he destroys them altogether?"

Zeus said: "You may do what you please."

Then they yoked the horses to Hera's chariot and went as fast as they could to the earth. Very fast they went, for every stride of the horses was over as much space as a man can see when he sits upon a cliff and looks over the sea to where the sky seems to come down upon it. When they came to the plain of Troy, they unharnessed the horses at a place where the two rivers met. They covered them and the chariot with a mist that no one might be able to see them, and they themselves flew as doves fly to where the Greeks and Trojans were fighting.

There Hera took the shape of Stentor, who could shout as loud as fifty men shouting at once, and cried: "Shame, men of Greece! when Achilles came to battle the Trojans scarcely dared to go beyond the gates of their city, but now they are driving you to your ships."

Athene went to Diomed, where he was standing and wiping away the blood from the wound which the arrow had made. "You are not like your father; he was a little man, but he was a great fighter. I do not know whether you are holding back because you are tired or because you are afraid; but certainly you are not like him."

Diomed knew who it was that was speaking to him, and answered: "Great goddess, I am not holding back because I am tired or because I am afraid. You yourself said to me: 'Do not fight against any god; only if Aphrodite comes into the battle, you may fight against her.' And this I have done. Her I wounded on the wrist and drove away; but when Apollo carried away Aeneas from me, then I held back. And now I see Ares rushing to and fro through the battle, and I do not dare to go against him."

Then said Athene: "Do not be afraid of Ares. I will come

with you, and you shall wound him with your spear, and drive him away from the battle."

She then pushed Diomed's charioteer with her hand, but the man did not see who it was that pushed him. And when he jumped down from the chariot she took his place, and caught the reins in her hand, and lashed the horses. Straight at Ares she drove, where he was standing by a Greek whom he had killed. Now Athene had put on her head the helmet of Hades, that is to say, of the god who rules the dead. Ares did not see her, for no one who wears the helmet can be seen. And he rushed at Diomed, thinking to kill him, and threw his spear with all his might.

But Athene put out her hand and turned the spear aside, so that it flew through the air and hurt no one. Then Diomed thrust his spear at Ares, and Athene leant all her weight upon it, so that it pierced the god just below the girdle. And when Ares felt the spear, he shouted with the pain as loud as an army of ten thousand men shouts when it goes forth to battle. And Diomed saw him rise up to the sky as a thunder-cloud arises.

And this was the greatest of the deeds of Diomed, that he wounded Ares, the god of war, and drove him out of the battle.

CHAPTER VIII

OF GLAUCUS AND DIOMED

Now the Trojans, in their turn, were driven back, for they could make no stand against the Greeks. There was one of the sons of King Priam who was a very wise prophet, and knew all that men should do to win the favour and help of the gods, and his name was Helenus. This man went up to Hector, and said to him and to Aeneas, who was standing near him: "Make the army fall back and get as close to the walls as may be, for it will be safer there than in the open plain. And go through the ranks, and speak to the men, and put as much courage into them as you can. And when you have done this, do you, Hector, go into the city, and tell your mother to gather together the daughters of Troy, and go with them to the temple of Athene, taking with her the most precious robe that she has, and lay the robe on the knees of the goddess, and promise to sacrifice twelve heifers, and beseech her to have pity on us and to keep this Diomed from the walls. Never did I see so fierce a man; even Achilles himself was not so terrible as he is, so dreadful is he and so fierce. Go, and come back as soon as you can, and we will do what we can to bear up against the Greeks while you are away."

So Hector went through the ranks, bidding the men be of good courage; and when he had done this he went into the city. And now the Trojans had a little rest. The way in which this happened shall now be told.

Sarpedon the Lycian had a cousin, Glaucus by name: the two were sons of brothers. This Glaucus, being one of the bravest of men, went in front of the Trojan line to meet Diomed. When Diomed saw him, he said: "Tell me, mighty man of valour, who you are, for I have never seen you before. This is a bold thing that you have done to come out in front of your comrades and to stand up against me. Truly those men whose children come in my way in battle are unlucky. Tell me then who you are, for if you are a god from heaven, then I will not fight with you. Already today have I done enough fighting with them, for it is an unlucky thing to do. King Lycurgus, in the land of Thrace, fought with a god, and it was a bad thing for him that he did so, for he did not live long. He drove Bacchus, the god of wine, into the sea. But the other gods were angry with him for this cause, and Zeus made him blind, and he perished miserably. But if you are no god, but a mortal man, then draw near that I may kill you with my spear."

Glaucus said: "Brave Diomed, why do you ask who I am, and who was my father, and my father's father? The generations of men are like the leaves on the trees. In the spring they shoot forth, and in the autumn they fall, and the wind blows them to and fro. And then when the spring comes others shoot forth, and these also fall in their time. So are the generations of men, one goes and another comes. Still, if you would hear of what race I come, listen. In a certain city of Greece which is called Corinth there dwelt a great warrior, Bellerophon by name. Someone spoke evil of this man falsely to the King of the city, and the King believed this false thing, and plotted his death. He was ashamed to kill him, but he sent him with a message to the King of Lycia. This message was written on a tablet, and the tablet was folded up in a cover, and the cover was sealed. But on the tablet was written: 'This is a wicked man; cause him to die.' So Bellerophon travelled to Lycia. And when he was come to the King's palace, the King made a great feast for him. For nine days did the feast last, and every day an ox was killed and eaten. On the morning of the tenth day the King said: 'Let me see the message which you have brought.' And when he had read it he thought how he might cause the man to die. First he sent him to conquer a great monster that there was in that country, called the Chimaera. Many men had tried to conquer it, but it had killed them all. It had the head of a lion, and its middle parts were those of a goat, and it had the tail of a serpent; and it breathed out flames of fire. This monster he killed, the gods helping him. Then the King sent him against a very fierce tribe of men, who were called the Solymi. These he conquered after much fighting, for, as he said himself, there never were warriors stronger than they. After this he fought with the Amazons, who were women fighting with the arms of men, and these also he conquered. And when he was coming back from fighting with the Amazons, the King set an ambush against him, choosing for it the bravest men in the whole land of Lycia. But Bellerophon killed them all, and came back safe to the King's palace. When the King saw this, he said to himself: 'The gods love this man; he cannot be wicked.' So he asked him about himself, and Bellerophon told him the whole truth. Then the King divided his kingdom with him, and gave him his daughter to wife. Three sons he had, of whom one was the father of Sarpedon and one was my father. And when my father sent me hither he said: 'Always seek to be the first, and to be worthy of those who have gone before.' This, then, brave Diomed, is the race to which I belong."

When Diomed heard this he was very glad, and said: "It is well that we did not fight, for we ought to be friends, as our fathers were before us. Long ago Aeneas entertained Bellerophon in his house. For twenty days he kept him. And when they parted they gave great gifts to each other, the one a belt embroidered with purple, and the other a cup of gold with a mouth on either side of it. Now Aeneas was my grandfather, as Bellerophon was yours. If then you should come to Corinth you will be my guest, and I will be yours if I go to the land of Lycia. But now we will not fight together. There are many Trojans and allies of the Trojans whom I may kill if I can overcome them, and there are many Greeks for you to fight with and to conquer, if you can. But we two will not fight together. And now let us exchange our armour, that all men may know that we are friends."

So the two chiefs jumped down from their chariots and exchanged their armour. And men said afterwards that Glaucus had lost his wits, for he gave armour of gold in exchange for armour of brass, armour that was worth a hundred oxen for armour that was worth nine only.

CHAPTER IX

HECTOR AND ANDROMACHE

When Hector passed through the gates into the city, hundreds of Trojan women crowded round him, asking what had happened to their sons or their husbands. But he said nothing to them, except to bid them pray that the gods would protect those whom they loved. When he came to the palace there met him his mother, Queen Hecuba. She caught him by the hand, and said: "O Hector, why have you come from the battle? Have the Greeks been pressing you hard? or have you come, maybe, to pray for help from Father Zeus? Let me bring a cup of wine, that you may pour out an offering to the god, aye, and that you may drink yourself and cheer your heart."

But Hector said: "Mother, give me no wine, lest it should make my knees weak, and take the courage out of my heart. Nor must I make an offering to the god with my hands unwashed. What I would have you do is this—gather the mothers of Troy together, and take the most beautiful and precious robe that you have, and go with them and lay it upon the knees of Athene, and pray to her to keep this terrible Diomed from the walls of Troy. And do not forget to promise a sacrifice of twelve heifers. And I will go and call Paris, and bid him come with me to the battle. Of a truth I could wish that the earth would open her mouth and swallow him up, for he is a curse to his father and to you his mother, and to the whole city of Troy."

Then Queen Hecuba went into her palace, and opened the store where she kept her treasures, and took out of it the finest robe that she had. And she and the noblest ladies that were in Troy carried it to the temple of Athene. Then the priestess, who was the wife of Antenor, received it from her hands, and laid it upon the knees of the goddess, making this prayer: "O Lady Athene, keeper of this city, break, we beseech thee, the spear of Diomed, and make him fall dead before the gates of Troy. If thou wilt have pity on the wives and children of the men of Troy, then we will offer to thee twelve heifers that have never been made to draw the plough."

So the priestess prayed; but Athene would not hear. And, indeed, it was she who had stirred up Diomed to fight so fiercely against Troy and had given him fresh strength and courage.

Meanwhile Hector went to the house of Paris. It stood on the citadel, close to his own house and to the palace of

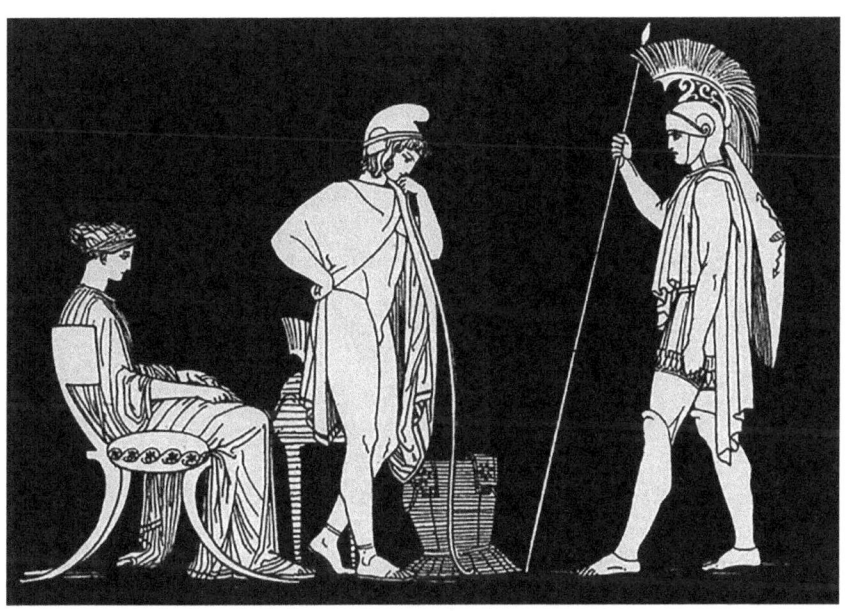

HECTOR CHIDING PARIS

King Priam. He found him cleaning his arms and armour, and the Fair Helen sat near him, with her maids, busy with needlework.

Then Hector thought to himself, "If I tell him that he went away from the battle because he was afraid, I shall offend him and do no good: I will try another way." So he said: "O Paris, is it right that you should stand aside and not fight in the battle because you are angry with your countrymen? The people perish, and the fight grows hotter and hotter every minute about the city. Rouse yourself and come forth before Troy is burnt up. For, remember, it is you that are the cause of all these troubles."

Then Paris answered: "O my brother, you have spoken well. But it was not because I was angry that I came away from the battle; it was because I was so much ashamed of being beaten. But now I will come back, for this is what my wife would have me to do; maybe I shall do better another time, for the gods give victory now to one man and now to another."

Then the Fair Helen said to Hector: "Sit down now and rest a little, for you must be very much tired with all that you have done."

But Hector answered: "You must not ask me to rest; I must make haste to help my countrymen, for indeed they are in sore need of help. But do you see that your husband overtakes me before I go out of the city gate. Now I am going to my house to see my wife and my little boy, for I do not know whether I shall ever see them again."

When he had said this, Hector went to his house to see his wife Andromache, for that was her name. But he did not find her at home, for she had gone to the wall, being very much afraid for her husband.

Hector asked the maids: "Where is the Lady Andromache? Has she gone to see one of her sisters-in-law, or, maybe, with the other mothers of Troy, to the temple of Athene?"

Then an old woman who was the housekeeper said: "Nay; she went to one of the towers of the wall that she might see the battle, for she had heard that the Greeks were pressing our people very much. She seemed like a madwoman, so much haste did she make, and the nurse went with her carrying the child."

Then Hector ran towards the gate, and Andromache saw him from where she stood on the wall, and made haste to meet him. And the nurse came after her, carrying the child, Hector's only son, a beautiful boy, with a head like a star, so bright was his golden hair. His father called him Scamandrius, after the river which runs across the plains of Troy; but the people called him Astyanax, which means the "City King," because it was his father who saved the city. And Hector smiled when he saw the child.

But Andromache did not smile, for she caught her husband by the hand, and wept, saying, "O Hector, your courage will be your death. You have no pity on your wife and child, and you do not spare yourself. Someday all the Greeks will join together and rush on you and kill you, and if I lose you, then it would be better for me to die than to live. I have no comfort but you. My father is dead; for the great Achilles killed him when he took our city. He killed him, but he did him great honour, for he would not take his arms for

THE MEETING OF HECTOR AND ANDROMACHE

THE PARTING OF HECTOR AND ANDROMACHE

a spoil, but burnt them with him; yes, and the nymphs of the mountains planted poplars by his grave. I had seven brothers, and they also are dead, for the great Achilles killed them all in one day. And my mother also is dead, for when her father had redeemed her with a great sum of money, Artemis slew her with one of her deadly arrows. But you are father to me and mother, and brother, and husband also. Have pity on me, and stay here upon the wall, lest you leave me a widow and your child an orphan. And set your people in order of battle by this fig tree, for here the wall is easier to attack. Here too, I see the bravest chiefs of the Greeks."

Hector answered her: "Dear wife, leave these things to me; I will look after them. One thing I cannot bear, that any son or daughter of Troy should see me skulking from the battle. I hate the very thought of it; I must always be in the front. Alas! I know that Priam and the people of Priam and this holy city of Troy will perish. But it is not for Troy, or for the people of Troy, nor even for my father and my mother, that I care so much; it is for you, when I think how some Greek will carry you away captive, and you will be set to spin or to carry water from the spring in a distant land. And some one will say: 'See that slave woman there! She was the wife of Hector, who was the bravest of the Trojans.'"

Then Hector stretched out his arms to take the child. But the child drew back into the bosom of his nurse, making a great cry, for he was frightened by the helmet which shone so brightly, and by the horsehair plume which nodded so awfully. And both his father and his mother laughed to hear him. Then Hector took the helmet from his head and laid it on the ground, and caught the boy in his hands, and kissed him and dandled him. And he prayed aloud to Father Zeus and to the other gods, saying:

"Grant, Father Zeus, and other gods who are in heaven, that this child may be as I am, a great man in Troy. And may the people say some day when they see him carrying home the bloody spoils of some enemy whom he has killed in battle: 'A better man than his father, this!' And his mother will be glad to hear it."

Then he gave the boy to his mother, and she clasped him to her breast and smiled, but there were tears in her eyes when she smiled. And Hector's heart was moved when he saw the tears; and he stroked her with his hand and said:

"Do not let these things trouble you. No man will be able to kill me, unless it be my fate to die. Fate no one may escape, whether he be a brave man or a coward. But go, dear wife, to your spinning again, and give your maids their tasks, and let the men see to the battle."

Then he took up the helmet from the ground, and put it on his head, and Andromache went to her home, but often, as she went, she turned her eyes to look at her husband. And when she came to her home she called all the maids together, and they wept and wailed for Hector as though he were already dead. And, indeed, she thought in her heart that she should never again see him coming home safe from the battle.

Hector went on his way to the gate, and as he went Paris came running after him. His arms shone brightly in the sun, and he himself went proudly along like a horse that is fresh from his stable, and prances over the grass and tosses his mane. And he said to Hector: "I am afraid that I have kept you when you were in a hurry to get back to your comrades."

Hector answered: "No man doubts that you are brave. But you are willful and hold back from the battle when you should be foremost. So it is that the people say shameful things about you. But now let us make haste to the battle."

So they went out by the gate, and fell upon the Greeks and killed many of them, and Glaucus the Lycian went with them.

CHAPTER X

HOW HECTOR AND AJAX FOUGHT

Athene was very sorry to see how her dear Greeks were being killed by Hector and his companions. So she flew down from the height of Olympus to see whether she could help them. When she had come to the plains of Troy she met Apollo. Now Apollo loved the Trojans, and he said to her: "Are you come, Athene, to help the Greeks whom you love? Now I, as you know, love the Trojans. Let us therefore join together and stop them from fighting for today. Hereafter they shall fight till that which the Fates have settled for Troy shall come to pass."

Athene answered: "How shall we stop them from fighting?" Apollo said: "We will set on Hector to challenge the bravest of the Greeks to fight with him, man to man."

So these two put the thought into the mind of the prophet Helenus. So Helenus went up to Hector and said: "Hector, listen to me. I am your brother, and also the gods have made me a prophet, so that you should take heed to the things which I say. Now my advice is this: cause the men of Troy and the Greeks to sit down in peace, and do you challenge the bravest of the enemy to fight with you, man to man. And be sure that in this fight you will not be killed, for so much the gods have told me, but whether you will kill the other, that I do not know, for the gods have not told me."

This pleased Hector greatly, and he went to the front of the army, holding his spear by the middle, and keeping the Trojans back. And King Agamemnon did the same with his own people. Then Hector said:

"Hear me, sons of Troy, and ye men of Greece. The covenant which we made together was broken. Truly this was not my doing; the gods would have it so, for it is their will that we should fight together, till either you take our city or we drive you to your ships, and compel you to go back to your own land. And yet listen to what I shall now say, for it may be that the gods will repent and suffer peace to be made between us. Do you Greeks choose out from those who are strongest and bravest among you someone to fight with me, man to man. And let this be agreed between us: if this man shall conquer me, then he shall take my arms for himself, but he shall give back my body to my people that they may burn it with fire. And, in like manner, if I shall conquer him, then I will take his arms for myself, but I will give his body to his people that they may bury it and raise a great mound over it. And so in days to come men who shall see it, as they sail by, will say: 'This is the tomb of the bravest of the Greeks, whom Hector of Troy killed in battle, fighting with him man to man.' So my name will be remembered for ever."

When the Greeks heard these words, they all stood still, saying nothing. They feared to meet the great Hector in battle, for he seemed to be stronger than he had ever been before, but they were ashamed to hold back. Then Menelaus jumped up in his place and cried: "Surely now ye are women and not men. What a shame it is to Greece that no one can be found to fight with this Hector! I will fight with him my own self, for the gods give the victory to one man or to another as they will."

So spoke Menelaus, for he was very angry, and did not care whether he lived or died. And, indeed, it would have been his death to fight with Hector, who was by much the stronger of the two. But King Agamemnon would not suffer him to be so rash. "Nay, my brother," he said, "this is but folly. Seek not to fight with one who is much stronger than you. Even Achilles was not willing to meet him. Sit still, therefore, for the Greeks will find some champion to meet him."

And Menelaus hearkened to his brother's words and sat down. But when no one stood up to offer himself to fight with Hector, old Nestor rose in his place and said: "Now this is a sad day for Greece! How sorry old Peleus would be to hear of this thing. I remember how glad he was when I told him about the chiefs who were going to fight against Troy, who they were and whence they came. And now he would hear that they all are afraid when Hector challenges them to fight with him man to man. He would pray that he might die. Oh, that I were such as I was in the old days, when the men of Pylos fought with the men of Arcadia. The men of Arcadia had a great champion, who was the strongest and biggest of all the men of that day, and carried the most famous arms in Greece, and a club of iron such as no one else could wield. And when this man challenged the men of Pylos to fight with him, the others, indeed, were afraid, for the man was like a giant; but I stood up, though I was the youngest of them all, and Athene stood by me and gave me great glory, for I slew him, and took from him his arms and his great iron club. Oh! that I were now such as I was that day! Hector would soon find someone to fight with him."

When old Nestor sat down, nine chiefs stood up. First among them was King Agamemnon, and after him Diomed and Ajax the Greater and Ajax the Less and Ulysses, and four others. Then said Nestor: "Let us cast lots to see who of these nine shall fight with Hector."

So the nine chiefs threw their lots, each man a lot, into the helmet of King Agamemnon. And the people standing round prayed silently to the gods: "Grant that the lot of Ajax the Greater may leap first out of the helmet, or the lot of Diomed, or the lot of King Agamemnon." Then Nestor shook the helmet, and it came to pass that the lot which first leapt forth was that very one which they most desired. For when the herald carried it round to the chiefs no one took it for his own, till the man came to Ajax the Greater. But Ajax had marked it with his own mark; he put out his hand, therefore, and claimed it. He was very glad in his heart, and he threw down the lot at his feet and cried: "The lot is mine, my friends, and I am glad above measure, for I think that I shall conquer this mighty Hector. And now I will put on my arms. And do you pray to Father Zeus, silently, if you will, that the Trojans may not hear; or if you had rather pray aloud, then do so, for I fear no man. None shall conquer me either by force or by craft, for the men of Salamis"—it was from the island of Salamis he came—"are not to be so conquered."

So Ajax put on his armour. And when he had finished, he went forward, as dreadful to look at as the god of war himself, and there was a smile on his face, but it was not the smile that other men like to see. Taking great strides he went, and he shook his great spear. And when the Trojans saw him their knees trembled beneath them, and even the great Hector felt that his heart beat more quickly than before. But he showed no fear, and stood firmly in his place, for he had himself challenged his adversary.

So Ajax came near, holding his great shield before him, as it might be a wall. There was no such shield in all the army of the Greeks. It had seven folds of bull's-hide, and one fold, the eighth, of bronze. Then Ajax spoke in a loud voice: "Come near, Hector, that you may see what men we have among us, we Greeks, though the great Achilles is not here, but sits idle in his tent."

Hector answered: "Do not speak to me, great Ajax, as though I were a woman or a child, and knew nothing of war. I know all the arts of battle, to turn my shield this way and that to meet the spear of the enemy, and to drive my chariot through the crowds of men and horses, and to fight hand to hand. But come, let us fight openly, face to face, as honest men should do."

As he spoke he threw his great spear at Ajax. Through six folds of bull's-hide it passed, but the seventh stopped it, for all that it was so strongly thrown. It was no easy thing to pierce the great shield with its seven folds. But when Ajax, in his turn, threw his spear at Hector, it passed through his shield, and through the armour that covered his body, and through the garment that was under the armour. It went near to killing him, but Hector bent his body away, and so saved himself. Then each took a fresh spear, and they ran together as fiercely as lions or wild boars. Again did Hector drive his spear against the great shield, and again did he drive it in vain, for the spear point was bent back. But Ajax, making a great leap from the ground, pierced Hector's shield with his spear, and pushed him back from the place where he stood, and the spear point grazed his neck, so that the blood spurted out. Then Hector caught up a great stone that lay upon the ground and threw it. And yet once more the great shield stayed him, nor could he break it through, and the great stone dropped upon the ground. But the stone which Ajax threw was heavier by far, and it broke Hector's shield and bore him to the ground, so that he lay on his back upon the ground, with the broken shield over him. Truly it had fared ill with him but that Apollo raised him up and set him on his feet. Then the two warriors drew their swords, but before they could get close together, the two heralds came up and thrust their staves between them. And the Trojan herald said: "It is enough, my sons; fight no more you are great warriors both of you, and Zeus loves you both. But now the night is at hand, and bids you cease, and you will do well to obey."

HECTOR AND AJAX SEPARATED BY THE HERALDS

HECTOR AND ANDROMACHE: THE FAREWELL

Then said Ajax: "Yes, herald; but it is for Hector to speak, for he began this matter, challenging the bravest of the Greeks to fight with him. And what he wills, that I will also."

Hector said: "The herald speaks well. Verily the gods have given you, O Ajax, stature and strength and skill. There is no better warrior among the Greeks. Let us cease then from fighting; haply we may meet again another day, and the gods may give the victory to you or to me. But now let us give gifts to each other, so that the Trojans and Greeks may say, 'Hector and Ajax met in battle, but parted in friendship.'"

Hector gave to Ajax a silver-studded sword, with a scabbard and a belt, and Ajax gave to Hector a buckler splendid with purple. So they parted. And the Trojans were right glad to see Hector coming back safe from the battle; on the other hand, the Greeks rejoiced yet more, for indeed their champion had prevailed. And King Agamemnon called all the chiefs to a feast, and to Ajax he gave the chine.[1] The Trojans also feasted in their city. But Zeus sent thunder all that night to be a sign of trouble to come.

---

[1] Editor's Note: A cut of meat that may include a part or all of the backbone.

CHAPTER XI

THE BATTLE ON THE PLAIN

When it was morning Zeus called all the gods and goddesses to an assembly on the top of Mount Olympus, and said to them: "Now listen to me, and obey. No one of you shall help either the Greeks or the Trojans; and mark this: if any god or goddess dares to do so I will throw him down from here into the outer darkness, and there he shall learn that I am lord in heaven. Does any one of you think that I am not stronger than you, yes than all of you put together? Well, let it be put to the trial. Let down a golden chain from heaven to earth, and take hold of it all of you, and see whether you can drag me from my throne. You cannot do it, not though you pull with all your might. But if I should choose to put out all my strength, I could lift you up, and the earth and the sea with you, and fasten the chain round one of the peaks of this mountain Olympus here, and leave you hanging in the air."

So did Zeus speak, and all the gods sat saying nothing, for they were terribly afraid. But at last Athene said: "Father, we know right well that none of us can stand up against you. And yet we cannot help pitying the Greeks, for we fear that they will be altogether destroyed. We will not help them, for this you forbid. But, if you will permit, we will give them advice."

And Zeus smiled, for Athene was his daughter, and he loved her better than any other among the gods and goddesses, and he gave his consent. Then he had his horses yoked to his chariot and touched them with his whip, and they flew midway between heaven and earth till they came to a certain mountain which was called Ida, and was near to Troy. There he sat down and watched the battle, for the time was come when he would keep the promise which he had made to Thetis.

The Greeks ate their food in haste and freshened themselves for battle; and the Trojans also armed themselves inside the city, and when they were ready the gates were opened and they went out. So the two armies came together, and shield was dashed against shield, and spear against spear, and there was a great clash of arms and shouting of men. So long as the sun was rising higher in the sky, neither of the two prevailed over the other; but at noon Zeus held out in the sky his golden scales, and in one scale he laid a weight for the Trojans and in the other a weight for the Greeks. Now the weights were weights of death, and the army whose weight was the heavier would suffer most. And lo! the scale of the Greeks sank lower.

Then Zeus sent a thunderbolt from the top of Mount Ida into the army of the Greeks, and there was great fear among both men and horses.

After this no man could hold his ground. Only old Nestor remained where he was, and he remained against his will, for Paris had killed one of his horses with an arrow, and the chariot could not be moved. So the old man began to cut away the traces, that he might free the horse that was yet alive from the horse that was dead. While he was doing this Hector came through the crowd of fighting men. Then had the old man perished, but Diomed saw it and went to help him. But first he called to Ulysses, whom he saw close by, running towards the ships. "Ulysses," he cried, as loudly as he could, "where are you going? Are you not ashamed to turn your back in this way like a coward? Take care that no man thrust you in the back with a spear and disgrace you forever. Stop now, and help me to save old Nestor from this fierce Hector."

So he spoke, but Ulysses gave no heed to his words, but still fled to the ships, for he was really afraid. When Diomed saw this he made haste, though he was alone, to go to the help of Nestor. When he got to the place where the old man was, he stopped his chariot and said: "Old friend, the young warriors are too much for you. Leave your own chariot for others to look after and climb into mine, and see what these horses of King Tros can do, for these are they which I took away from Aeneas. There are none faster, or better, or easier to turn this way or that. Take these reins in your hand, and I will go against this Hector, and see whether the spear of Diomed is as strong as it was of old."

So old Nestor climbed up into the chariot, and took the reins in his hand and touched the horses with the whip, driving straight at Hector. And when they were near him, Diomed threw his spear at him. Him he missed, but he struck down his charioteer, and the man fell dead to the ground. Hector was greatly grieved, but he let him lie where he fell, for he must needs find another man to drive the horses. And when he went back from the front to look for the man, then the Trojans went back also, for it was Hector to whom they looked and whom they followed. But when Diomed would have pursued them, Zeus threw another thunderbolt from Ida. It fell right in front of the chariot, and the horses crouched on the ground for fear, and Nestor let the reins drop from his hand, for he was greatly afraid, and cried: "O Diomed, let us fly; see you not that Zeus is against us? He gives glory to Hector today, tomorrow, maybe, he will give it to you. But what he wills that will he do, and no man may hinder him."

Diomed answered: "Old sir, you speak wisely. Yet it goes to my heart to turn back. For Hector will say, 'Diomed fled before me, seeking to hide himself in the ships.' I had sooner that the earth should open her mouth and swallow me up, than that I should hear such things."

But Nestor answered: "O Diomed, be content: though Hector may call you coward, the sons of Troy will not believe him, no, nor the daughters of Troy, whose brothers and husbands you have tumbled in the dust."

So then he turned the horses to fly. And Hector cried when he saw the great Diomed fly before him: "Are you the man to whom the Greeks give the chief place in their feasts and great cups of wine? They will not so honour you after today. Run, girl! run, coward! Are you the man that was to climb our walls and carry away our people captive?"

Diomed was very angry to hear these words, and doubted whether he should flee or turn again to the battle. But as he doubted, Zeus made a great thundering in the sky, and he was afraid. Then Hector called to his horses; by their names he called them, saying, "Come, Whitefoot and Bayard and Brilliant and Flame of Fire; remember how the fair Andromache has cared for you, putting you even before me, who am her husband. Carry me now as fast as you can, that I may take from old Nestor his shield, which men say is made all of gold, and from Diomed his breastplate, which was wrought for him in the forge of heaven."

So the Greeks fled as fast as they could within the wall which they had built for a defence for their ships, for Hector drove them before him, nor was there one who dared to stand up against him. And the space between the wall and the ships was crowded with chariots, and no spirit was left in any man. Then Hera put into the heart of King Agamemnon that he should encourage his people to turn again to battle. So the King stood by the ship of Ulysses, which was in the middle of the ships, for they were drawn up in a long line upon the shore, and cried aloud: "Shame on you, Greeks! Where are your boats which you boasted before you came to this land, how that one of you would be more than a match for a hundred, yea, for two hundred Trojans? It was easy to say such words when you ate the flesh of bullocks and drank full cups of wine. But now, when you are put to the trial, a single Trojan is worth more than you all. Was there ever a king who had such cowards for his people?"

Then the Greeks took courage and turned again, and set upon the Trojans. And the first of all to turn and to slay a Trojan was Diomed. He drove his spear through the man's back, for now the Trojans were flying in their turn, and tumbled him from his chariot. And after Diomed came King Agamemnon, and Ajax, and other chiefs. Among them was Teucer, the brother of Ajax, a skilful archer. He stood under the shield of his brother, and Ajax would lift the shield a little, and then Teucer would peer out and take aim and send an arrow at some Trojan, and kill him or wound him. Then he would go back, as a child runs to his mother, and Ajax covered him with his shield. Eight warriors did he hit in this way. And when King Agamemnon saw him, he said: "Shoot on, Teucer, and be a joy to your people and to your father. Surely when we have taken the city of Troy, and shall divide the spoil, you shall have the best gift of all after mine."

And Teucer said: "I need no gifts, O King, to make me eager. I have not ceased to shoot my arrows at these Trojans; eight arrows have I shot, and every one has found its way through some warrior's armour into his flesh. But this Hector I cannot hit."

And as he spoke he let fly another arrow at Hector from the sling. Him he did not touch, but he slew a son of Priam. And then he shot yet a tenth, and this time he laid low the charioteer who stood by Hector's side. Then Hector's heart was filled with rage and grief. He leant down from his chariot, and caught up a great stone in his hand, and ran at Teucer, that he might crush him to the earth. And Teucer, when he saw him coming, made haste, and took an arrow from his quiver and fitted it to the sling. But even as he drew back the string to his shoulder, the great stone struck him where the collar-bone stands out between the neck and the arm. It broke the bow-string, and made his arm and wrist all weak and numb, so that he could not hold the bow. And he fell upon his knees, dropping the bow upon the ground. But Ajax stood over him, and covered him with his shield, and two of his comrades took him up in their arms and carried him, groaning deeply, to the ships.

When the Trojans saw the great archer carried away from the battle, they took fresh courage, and drove back the Greeks to the ditch, for there was a ditch in front of the wall. And Hector was always in the very front. As a dog follows a wild beast and catches him by the hip or the thigh as he flies, so did Hector follow the Greeks and slay the hindmost of them.

Then Hera, as she sat on the top of Olympus, said to Athene: "Shall we not have pity on the Greeks and help them? Let us do it this once if we never do it again. I fear much that they will perish altogether by the hand of Hector. See what harm he has done to them already."

Athene answered: "This is also my Father's doing. He listened to Thetis when she asked him to do honour to her son Achilles. But, perhaps, he may now listen to me, and will let me help the Greeks. Make your chariot ready, therefore, and I will put on my armour. So we will go together to the battle; maybe that. Hector will not be glad when he sees us coming against him."

So Hera made her chariot ready, and Athene put on her armour, and took her great spear, and prepared as for battle.

Then the two mounted the chariot, and the Hours opened the gates of heaven for them, and they went towards Troy.

Zeus saw them from where he sat on the top of Mount Ida. And he called to Iris, who is the messenger of the gods, and said to her: "Go now, Iris, and tell these two that they had better not set themselves against me. If they do, then I will lame their horses, and throw them down from their chariot, and break the chariot in pieces. If I do but strike them with my thunderbolt, they will not recover from their hurts for ten years and more."

Iris made all the haste she could, and met the two goddesses on their way, and gave them the message of Zeus. When Hera heard it, she said to Athene: "It is not wise for us two to fight with Zeus for the sake of men. Let them live or die, as he may think best, but we will not set ourselves against him."

Hera turned the chariot, and they went back to Olympus, and sat down in their chairs of gold among the other gods. Very sad and angry were they.

When Zeus saw that they had gone back, he left Mount Ida and went to Olympus, and came into the hall where the gods were assembled. When he saw Hera and Athene sitting by themselves with gloomy faces, he mocked them, saying: "Why do you look so sad? Surely it cannot be that you have tired yourselves by joining in the battle, and slaying these Trojans whom you hate so much? But if it is because the thing that I will does not please you, then know that what I choose to happen, that shall happen. Yes; if all the other gods should join together against me, still I shall prevail over them."

HERA AND ATHENE GOING TO ASSIST THE GREEKS

When Zeus had so spoken, then Athene, for all that her heart was bursting with anger, said nothing; but Hera would not keep silence. "Well do we know, O Zeus, that you are stronger than all the gods. Nevertheless we cannot but pity the Greeks when we see them perishing in this way."

Zeus spake again: "Is it so? Do you pity the Greeks for what they have suffered to-day? To-morrow you shall see worse things than these, O Queen. For Hector will not cease from driving the Greeks before him and slaying them till the great Achilles himself shall be moved, and shall rise from his place where he sits by his ships."

And now the sun sank into the sea, and the night fell. The Trojans were angry that the darkness had come and that they could not see any longer but the Greeks were glad of the night, for it was as a shelter to them, and gave them time to breathe.

Then Hector called the Trojans to an assembly at a place that was near the river, where the ground was clear of dead bodies. He stood up in the middle of the people, holding in his hand a spear, sixteen feet or more in length, with a shining head of bronze, and a band of gold by which the head was fastened to the shaft. What he said to the people was this: "Hearken, men of Troy, and ye, our allies who have come to help us. I thought that to-day we should destroy the army of the Greeks and burn their ships, and so go back to Troy and live in peace. But night has come, and hindered us from finishing our work. Let us sit down, therefore, and rest, and take a meal. Loose your horses from your chariots and give them their food. Go, some of you, to the city, and fetch from thence cattle, and sheep, and wine, and bread that we may have plenty to eat and drink: also fetch fuel, that we may burn fires all the night, that we may sit by them, and also that we see whether the Greeks will try to escape in the night. Truly they shall not go in peace. Many will we kill, and the rest shall, at the least, carry away with him a wound for him to heal at home, that so no man may come again and trouble this city of Troy. The heralds also shall go to the city and make a proclamation that the old men and the boys shall guard the wall, and that every woman shall light a hearth fire, and that all shall keep watch, lest the enemy should enter the city, while the people are fighting at the ships. And now I will say no more but to-morrow I shall have other words to speak to you. But know this, that to-morrow we will arm ourselves, and drive these Greeks to their ships; and, if it may be, burn these ships with fire. Then shall we know whether the bold Diomed shall drive me back from the wall or whether he shall be himself slain with the spear. To-morrow shall surely bring ruin on the Greeks. I would that I were as sure of living for ever and ever, and of being honoured as the gods are honoured."

Thus Hector spoke, and all the Trojans shouted with joy to hear such words. Then they unharnessed the horses, and fetched provender for them from the city, and also gathered a great store of fuel. They sat all night in hope of what the next day would bring. As on a calm night the stars shine bright, so shone the watch-fires of the Trojans. A thousand fires were burning, and by each fire sat fifty men. And the horses stood by the chariots champing oats and barley. So they all waited for the morning.

CHAPTER XII

THE REPENTANCE OF AGAMEMNON

While the Trojans made merry, being full of hope that they would soon be rid of their enemies, the Greeks, on the other hand, were full of trouble and fear. Not one of them was more sad at heart than King Agamemnon. After a while he called the heralds and told them to go round to the chiefs and bid them come to a council. "Bid them one by one," he said, "and do not proclaim the thing publicly, for I would not have the people know of it." So the chiefs came, and sat down each man in his seat. Not a word did they say, but looked sadly on the ground. At last King Agamemnon stood up and spoke: "O my friends, lords and rulers of the Greeks, truly Zeus seems to hate me. Once he promised me that I should take this city of Troy and return home in safety, but this promise he has not kept. I must go back to the place from which I came without honour, having lost many of those who came with me. But now, before we all perish, let us flee in our ships to our own land, for Troy we may not take."

When the King had finished his speech the chiefs still sat saying not a word, for they were out of heart. But after a while, seeing that no one else would speak, brave Diomed stood up in his place and said: "O King, do not be angry, if I say that this talk of yours about fleeing in our ships to our own land is nothing but madness. It was but two days since that you called me a coward, and whether this be true the Greeks, both young and old, know well. I will not say 'yes' or 'no.' But this I tell you. Zeus has given you to be first among the Greeks, and to be a king among kings. But courage he has not given you, and courage is the best gift of all, and without it all others are of no account. Now, if you are bent on going back, go; your ships are ready to be launched, and the way is short; but all the other Greeks will stay till they have taken the city of Troy. Aye, and if they also choose to go with you, still I will stay, I and Sthenelus here, my friend: yes we two will stay, and we will fight till we make an end of the city, for the gods sent us hither, and we will not go back till we have done the thing for which we came."

Then old Nestor stood up in his place and said: "You are a brave man, O Diomed, and you speak words of wisdom. There is not a man here but knows that you have spoken the truth. And now, O King Agamemnon, do you seek counsel from the chiefs, and when they have spoken, follow that counsel which shall seem to you wisest and best. But first let them sit down to eat and to drink, for they have toiled all day in the battle, and it is your part to give them meat and drink. Also set sentinels to keep watch along the trench lest our enemies should fall upon us unawares, for they have many watch-fires and a mighty host. Verily this night will either save us or make an end of us altogether."

The King then bade his men prepare a feast, and the chiefs sat down to eat and drink; and when they had had enough, Nestor rose up in his place and spoke: "O King, Zeus has made you lord over many nations, and put many things into your hand. Therefore you have the greater need of good counsel, and are the more bound to listen to wise words, even though they may not please you. It was an evil day, O King, when you sent the heralds to take away the damsel Briseis from Achilles. The other chiefs did not consent to your deed. Yes, and I myself advised you not to do this thing; but you would not hear. Rather you followed your own pride and pleasure, and shamed the bravest of your followers, taking away from him the prize which he had won with his own hands. Do you, therefore, undo this evil deed, and make peace with this man whom you have wronged, speaking to him pleasant words and giving him noble gifts."

King Agamemnon stood up and said: "You have spoken true words, old sir. Truly I acted as a fool that day; I do not deny it. For not only is this Achilles a great warrior but he is dear to Zeus, and he that is dear to Zeus is worth more than whole armies of other men. See now how we are put to flight when he stands aside from the battle! This surely is the doing of Zeus. And now, as I did him wrong, so I will make him amends, giving him many times more than that which I took from him. Hear now the gifts which I will give him: seven kettles, standing on three feet, new, which the fire has never touched, ten talents of gold, and twenty bright caldrons, and twelve strong horses which have won many prizes for me by their swiftness. The man who had as much gold of his own as these twelve horses have won for me would not be a beggar. Also I will give him some women-slaves, skilled with their needle and in other work of the hands, who were my portion of the spoil, when we took the island of Lesbos. Yes, and I will send back to him the maiden Briseis, whom I took from him. And when, by favour of the gods, we shall have taken the city of Troy, and shall divide the spoil, then let him come and choose for himself twenty women the most beautiful that there are in the city, after the Fair Helen, for none can be so beautiful as she. And I will give him yet more than this. When we get back to the land of Greece, then he shall be as a son to me, and I will honour him even as I honour my own son Orestes. Three daughters have I in my palace at home. Of these he shall have the one whom he shall choose for his wife, and shall take her to the house of his father Peleus. Nor shall he give any gifts, as a man is used to give when he seeks a maiden for his wife. He shall have my daughter without a price. And more than this, I will give with her a great dowry, such as king has never given before to his daughter. Seven fair cities will I give him, and with each city fields in which many herds of oxen and flocks of sheep are grazing, and vineyards out of which much wine is made. And the people of these cities shall honour him as their lord and master. All these things will I give him, if only he will cease from his anger. Let him listen to our prayers, for of all things that are in the world there is but one that does not listen to prayers, and this one thing is Death. And this, verily, is the cause why Death is hated of all men. Let him not therefore be as Death."

When Agamemnon had made an end of speaking, Nestor said to him: "The gifts which you are ready to give to the great Achilles are such as no man can find fault with. Let us, therefore, without delay, choose men who may go to his tent and offer them to him. Let Phoenix go first, for he is dear to the gods, and Achilles also honours him, for, indeed, Phoenix had the care of him when he was a child. And with him Ajax the Greater should go, and Ulysses also, and let two heralds go with them. And now let the heralds bring water and pour upon our hands, and let each keep silence, while we pray to Zeus that he may have mercy upon us, and incline the heart of this man to listen to our entreaties."

Then the heralds brought water, and poured it upon the hands of the chiefs, and they filled the bowls with wine. And each man took his bowl and poured out a little on the ground, praying meanwhile to the gods. And when they had done this, they drank, and came out from the King's tent. And, before they went on their errand, old Nestor charged them what they should say. All of them he charged, but Ulysses most of all, because he was the best speaker of them all.

CHAPTER XIII

THE EMBASSY TO ACHILLES

So they went along the shore of the sea, and as they went they prayed to the god who shakes the earth, that is to say, the god of the sea, that he would shake the heart of Achilles. And when they came to the camp of the Myrmidons, for these were the people of Achilles, they saw the King with a harp in his hand, the harp he had taken from the city of Thebe (which was also the city of Andromache). He was playing on the harp, and as he played he sang a song about the valiant deeds which the heroes of old time had wrought. And Patroclus sat over against him in silence, waiting till he should have ended his singing. So the three chiefs came forward, Ulysses leading the way, and stood before Achilles. And he, when he saw them, jumped up from his seat, not a little astonished, holding his harp in his hand.

And Patroclus also rose up from his seat, to do them honour. And Achilles said: "You are welcome, my friends: though I am angry with the King, you are not the less my friends."

When he had said this he bade them sit down upon chairs that were there, covered with coverlets of purple. And to Patroclus he said: "Bring out the biggest bowl, and mix the wine and make it as strong and sweet as you can and give to each of these my friends a cup that they may drink, for there are none whom I love more in the whole army of the Greeks."

This Patroclus did. And when he had mixed the wine, strong and sweet, and had given to each man his cup, then he made ready a feast. Nor were they unwilling, though they had but just feasted in the tent of King Agamemnon, for the men of those days were as mighty in eating and drinking as in fighting. And the way that he made ready the feast was this. First he put a great block of wood as close as might be to the fire. And on this he put the back, that is to say, the saddle of a sheep, and the same portion of a fatted goat, and also the same of a well-fed pig. The charioteer of Achilles held the flesh in its place with a spit, and Achilles carved it. And when he had carved the portions, he put each on a skewer. Then Patroclus made the fire burn high, and when the flames had died down, then he smoothed the red-hot embers, and put racks upon the top of them, and on the racks, again, the spits with the flesh. But first he sprinkled them with salt. And when the flesh was cooked, he took it from the skewers, and put portions of it on the platters. Also he took bread and put it in baskets, to each man a basket. Then they all took their places for the meal, and Achilles gave the place of honour to

Ulysses. Before they began, he signed to Patroclus that he should sacrifice to the gods, and this he did by casting into the fire something of the flesh and of the bread. After this they put forth their hands, and took the food that was ready for them.

When they had had enough, Ajax nodded to Phoenix, meaning that he should speak and tell Achilles why they had come. But Ulysses perceived it, and he began to speak before Phoenix. First he filled a cup, and drank to the health of Achilles, and then he said: "Hail, Achilles! Truly we have had no lack of feasting, first in the tent of King Agamemnon, and now in yours. But this is not a day to think of feasting, for destruction is close at hand, and we are greatly afraid. This very day the Trojans and their allies came very near to burning our ships and we are greatly in doubt whether we shall save them, for it is plainly to be seen that Zeus is on their side. What, therefore, we are come to ask of you is that you will not stand aside any longer from the battle, but will come and help us as of old. And truly our need is great. For this Hector rages furiously, saying that Zeus is with him, and not caring for god or man. And even now he is praying that morning may appear, for he vows that he will burn the ships with fire and destroy us all while we are choked with the smoke of the burning. And I am greatly afraid that the gods will give him strength to make good his threats and to kill us all here, far away from the land in which we were born. Now, therefore, stir yourself if now, before it is too late, you have a mind to save the Greeks. Make no delay, lest it be too late, and you repent only when that which is done shall be past all recalling. Did not the old man Peleus, your father, on the day when he sent you from Phthia, your country, to follow King Agamemnon, lay this charge upon you, saying: 'My son, the gods will give you strength and will make you mighty in battle, if it be their will but there is something which you must do for yourself: keep down the pride of your heart, for gentleness is better than pride also keep from strife, so shall the Greeks, both young and old, love you and honour you?' This charge your father laid upon you, but you have not kept it. Nevertheless there is yet a place of repentance for you. For the King has sent us to offer you gifts great and many to make up for the wrong that he did to you. So great and so many are they that no one can say that these are not worthy."

Then Ulysses set forth in order all the things which Agamemnon had promised to give, kettles and caldrons and gold, and women slaves, and his daughter in marriage, and seven cities to be her dowry. And when he had finished the list of these things he said: "Be content: take these gifts, which, indeed, no man can say are not sufficient. And if you have no thought for Agamemnon, yet you should have thought for the people who perish because you stand aside from the battle. Take the gifts, therefore, for by so doing you will have wealth and love and honour from the Greeks, and great glory also, for you will slay Hector, who is now ready to meet you in battle, so proud is he, thinking that there is not a man of all the Greeks who can stand against him."

Achilles answered: "I will speak plainly, O Ulysses, and will set out clearly what I think is in my heart, and what I intend to do. It does not please me that you should sit there and coax me, one man saying one thing and another man saying another. Yes, I will speak both plainly and truly, for,

THE EMBASSY TO ACHILLES

THE EMBASSY TO ACHILLES

as for the man who thinks one thing in his heart and says another thing with his tongue, he is hateful to me as death itself. Tell me now, what does it profit a man to be always fighting day after day? It is but thankless work, for the man that stays at home has an equal share with the man who never leaves the battle, and men honour the coward even as they honour the brave, and death comes alike to the man that works and to the man who sits idle at home. Look now at me! What profit have I had of all that I have endured, putting my life in peril day after day? Even as a bird carries food to its nestlings till they are fledged, and never ceases to work for them, and herself is but ill fed, so it has been with me. Many nights have I been without sleep, and I have laboured many days. I took twelve cities to which I travelled in ships, and eleven to which I went by land, and from all I carried away much spoil. All this spoil I brought to King Agamemnon, and he, who all the time had stayed safe in his tent, gave a few things to me and to others, but kept the greater part for himself. And then what did he do? He left to the other chiefs that which he had given to them, but what he had given to me, that he took from me. Yes; he took Briseis. Let him keep her, if he will. But let him not ask me any more to fight against the Trojans. There are other chiefs whom he has not wronged and shamed in this way; let him go to them and take counsel with them, how he may keep away the devouring fire from the ships. Many things he has done already; he has built a wall, and dug a ditch about it; can he not keep Hector from the ships with them? And yet in time past when I used to fight, this Hector dared not set his army in array far from the walls of Troy; nay, he scarce ventured to come outside the gates. Once indeed

did he gather his courage together and stand up against me,
to fight man with man, and then he barely escaped from my
spear. But neither with him nor with any other of the sons of
Troy will I fight again. To-morrow I will do sacrifice to Zeus
and the other gods, and I will store my ships with food and
water, and launch them on the sea. Yes, early in the morning
to-morrow, if you care to look, you will see my ships upon
the sea, and my men rowing with all their might. And, if the
god of the sea gives me a good passage, on the third day I
shall come to my own dear country, even to Phthia. There are
the riches which I left behind me when I came to this land
of Troy, and thither shall I carry such things, gold and silver
and slaves, as King Agamemnon has not taken from me. But
with him I will never take counsel again, nor will I stand by
his side in battle. As for his gifts, I scorn them; aye, and were
they twenty times as great, I would scorn them still. Not with
all the wealth of Thebes which is in the land of Egypt would
he persuade me, and than Thebes there is no wealthier city in
all the world. A hundred gates it has, and through each gate
two hundred warriors ride forth to battle with chariots and
horses. And as for his daughter whom he would give me to be
my wife, I would not marry her, no, not though she were as
beautiful as Aphrodite herself, and as skilled in all the works
of the needle as Athene. Let him choose for his son-in-law
some chief of the Greeks who is better than I am. As for me,
if the gods suffer me to reach my home, my father Peleus
shall choose me a wife. Many maidens, daughters of kings,
are there in Phthia and in Hellas, and not one among them
who would scorn me if I came a-wooing. Often in time past
have I thought to do this thing, to marry a wife, and to settle

down in peace, and to enjoy the riches of the old man my father, and such things as I have gathered for myself. For long since my mother, Thetis of the sea, said to me, 'My son, there are two lots of life before you, and you may choose which you will. If you stay in this land and fight against Troy, then you must never go back to your own land, but will die in your youth. Only your name will live forever; but if you will leave this land and go back to your home, then shall you live long, even to old age, but your name will be forgotten.' Once I thought that fame was a better thing than life; but now my mind is changed, for indeed my fame is taken from me, seeing that King Agamemnon puts me to shame before all the people. And now I go away to my own land, and I counsel you to go also, for Troy you will never take. The city is dear to Zeus, and he puts courage into the hearts of the people. And take this answer back to the man who sent you: 'Find some other way of keeping Hector and the Trojans from the ships, for my help he shall not have.' But let Phoenix stay with me this night, that he may go with me in my ship when I depart to-morrow. Nevertheless if he choose rather to stay, let him stay, for I would not take him by force."

When Achilles had ended his speech, all the chiefs sat silent, so vehement was he.

CHAPTER XIV

THE STORY OF OLD PHOENIX

Old Phoenix stood up and spoke, and as he spoke he shed many tears, for he was much afraid lest the ships of the Greeks should be burnt. "O Achilles," he said, "if you are indeed determined to go away, how can I stay here without you? Did not the old man Peleus, your father, make me your teacher, that I might show you both what you should say and what you should do, when he sent you from the land of Phthia to be with King Agamemnon? In those days, for all that you are now so strong and skilful in war, you were but a lad, knowing nothing of how warriors fight in battle, or of how they take counsel together. No: I cannot stay here without you I would not leave you, no, not if the gods would make me young again as when I came to the land of Phthia, to be with Peleus your father. For at the first I lived in Hellas, and left it because the old man, my father, was angry with me. So angry was he that he cursed me, and prayed to Zeus and the other gods that no child of mine should ever sit upon his knees. And I, too, was very angry when I heard him say these words. Truly the thought came into my heart that I would fall upon him and slay him with the sword. But the gods were merciful to me and helped me to put away this wicked thought out of my heart. So I gave up my anger, for I could not bear that men should say of me: 'See, there is the man who killed his own father!' But I was determined to go away from my father's house and from the land of Hellas altogether. Then came my friends and my kinsmen, and made many prayers to me, beseeching me that I would not depart. But I would not listen to them. Then they would have kept me by force. Nine days and nine nights they watched in my father's house, eating the flesh of sheep and oxen and swine, and drinking wine without stint from my father's stores. They took turns to watch, and they kept up two fires without ceasing, one in the cloister that was round the house, and one before the great door. But on the tenth night, when the watchmen were overcome with sleep and the fires were low, then I broke open the door of my chamber, for all that they had shut it fast with a knot that was hard to untie, and I leapt over the fence of the courtyard, and neither man nor maid saw me. So I escaped, and fled from Hellas, and came to Phthia to the old man Peleus your father. And your father was very kind to me, and was as a father to me. He gave me riches, and he gave me a kingdom which I might rule under him, and also he trusted you to me, O Achilles, when you were but a little child, that I might teach you and rear you. And this I did. And, indeed, you loved me much. With no one but me would you go into the hall or sit at the feast. I would hold you on my knees and carve the choicest bits for you from the dish, and put the wine-cup to your lips. Many a time have you spoilt my clothes sputtering out the wine from your lips, when I had put the cup to your lips. Yes, I suffered much, and toiled much for you, and you were as a child to me, for child of my own I never had. And now, I pray you, listen to me. Put away the anger out of your heart even as I put the anger out of mine. It is not fit that a man should harden his heart in this way. Even the gods are turned from their purpose, and surely the gods are more honourable and more powerful than you. Yet men turn them by the offering of incense and by drink-offerings and by burnt-offerings and by prayers. And if a man sins against them yet can he turn them from their anger. For, indeed, Prayers are the daughters of Zeus. They are weak and slow of foot, whereas Sin is swift and strong, and goes before, running over all the earth, and doing harm to men. But nevertheless they come after and heal the harm that Sin has done. If, therefore, a man will reverence these daughters of Zeus, and will do honour to them when they come near to him, and will listen to their voice, they will bless him and do good to him. But if a man hardens his heart against them and will not listen to their voice, then they curse him and bring him to ruin. Take heed, therefore, O Achilles, that thou do such honour to those daughters of Zeus as becomes a righteous man, for it will be well for you to do so. If, indeed, King Agamemnon had stood apart and given you no gifts, nor restored to you that which he took from you, then I would not have bidden you

cease from your anger, no, not to save the Greeks from their
great trouble. But now he gives you many gifts, and promises
you yet more, and has sent an embassy to you, the wisest and
noblest that there are in the whole army, and also dear friends
of yours. Refuse not, therefore, to listen to their words.
Listen now to this tale that I will tell you, that you may see
how foolish a thing it is for a man, however great he may be,
to shut his ears when prayers are made to him.

"Once upon a time there was a great strife between the
Ætolians and the men who dwelt near to Mount Curium.
And the cause of the strife was this. There was a great wild
boar which laid waste all the land of Calydon where the
Ætolians dwelt. And Meleager, who was the King of the land,
sent for hunters from all Greece, and they came from far and
wide, bringing their dogs with them, for the beast was so great
and fierce that it was not an easy thing to kill it, but there
was need of many hunters. Now, among those that came was
Atalanta, the fair maid of Arcadia. And when the beast was
killed, then there was a great quarrel as to who should have
the spoils, that is to say the head and the hide. For Meleager
gave them to the fair Atalanta, and when the brethren of his
mother took them from her, then he slew them. But when
his mother, Althea by name, heard that her brethren were
dead, then she cursed him, yea, even her own son. So it came
to pass that there was war between the Ætolians and the men
of Mount Curium, for Althea and her brethren were of that
land. And also the curse began to work so that the quarrel
became more fierce. Now, when in time past Meleager had
fought among the Ætolians there was none that could stand
up against him, so great a warrior was he. But now, being

very angry with his mother, he stood aside from the war, and would not help, sitting in his chamber apart. The men of Mount Curium, therefore, prevailed in the battle, and the Ætolians were driven into the city of Calydon, and there was a din of war about the gates of the city, and great fear lest the enemy should break them down. Then first the elders of the city sent an embassy to him, priests of the gods, the holiest that there were in the land, to pray that he would come forth from his chamber and defend them. Also they promised him a noble gift, a great estate in the plain of Ætolia, half plough-land and half vineyard, such as he might choose for him-self. So the priests came, beseeching him, and offering him the gift, but he would not listen to them. After them came his mother and his sisters, and made their prayers to him, but them he refused even more fiercely. And the old man Œneus,[1] his father, besought him, standing on the threshold of his chamber, and shaking the door; but he would not listen. Nor would he hear the voice of his friends and com-rades, although they were very dear to him. But at the last, when the enemy had now begun to climb upon the towers, and to burn the fair city of Calydon with fire, aye and to batter on the doors of his palace, then his wife, the fair Cleopatra, arose and besought him with many prayers and tears. 'Think now,' she said, 'what woes will come upon your people if the enemy prevail against them, for the city will be burnt with fire, and the men will be slain, and the women

---

[1] Editor's Note: "Œ" - a ligature of o and e. Ligatures were used for English words with Greek and Latin origins and to prevent character collisions in type. The most common ligature in modern English is the ampersand: "&".

will be carried into captivity.' Then at last his spirit was stirred within him, and he arose, and put on his arms, and went down into the street, and drove the men of Mount Curium before him. So did he save the Ætolians, but the gifts which they promised, these he never had. This, O Achilles, is the story of Meleager. Let not your thoughts be like to his. It would be a foolish thing to put off the saving of the ships till they are already on fire. Come, therefore, take the gifts which King Agamemnon gives you so shall all the Greeks honour you even as they honour a god. But if you delay, then may you lose both honour and gifts, even though you save us from the Trojans."

Achilles answered: "Phoenix, my father, I have no need of this honour and these gifts. Riches I have as much as I need, and Zeus gives me honour. And listen to this: trouble me no more with prayers and tears, while you seek to help King Agamemnon. Take not his side, lest I, who love you now, come to hate you. It were better for you to vex him who has vexed me. Return now with me to the land of Phthia, and I will give you the half of my kingdom. And stay this night in my tent; to-morrow we will consult together whether we will depart or no."

Then Achilles nodded to Patroclus, and made signs that he should make a bed ready for the old man, so that the other two, seeing this, should depart without delay.

So Patroclus made the bed ready. And when Ajax saw this he said to Ulysses: "Let us go, Ulysses. We shall do nothing to-day. Let us, therefore, depart at once, and carry back this message to them who sent us. As for Achilles, he cherishes his anger, and cares nought for his comrades or his people. What he desires, I know not. One man will take the price of blood from another, even though he has slain a brother or a son. He takes the gold, and puts away his anger, and the shedder of blood dwells in peace in his own land. But this man keeps his anger, and all for the sake of a girl. And lo! the King offers him seven girls, yea seven for one, and he will not take them. Surely he seems to lack reason."

Achilles answered: "You speak well, great Ajax. Nevertheless the anger is yet hot in my heart, because Agamemnon put me to shame before all the people, as if I were but a common man. But go, and take my message. I will not arise to do battle with the Trojans till Hector shall come to these tents and shall seek to set fire to my ships. But when he shall do this, then I will arise, and verily I will stop him, however eager he may be for the battle."

So Ajax and Ulysses departed, and gave the message of Achilles to King Agamemnon.

CHAPTER XV

THE ADVENTURE OF DIOMED AND ULYSSES

While the other chiefs of the Greeks were sleeping that night, King Agamemnon was awake, for he had great trouble in his heart and many fears. When he looked towards Troy he saw the fires burning, and heard the sound of flutes and pipes, and the murmurs of many men, and he was astonished, for it seemed to him that the army of the Trojans was greater and stronger than it had ever been in time past. And when he looked towards the ships, he groaned and tore his hair, thinking what evils might come to the people. Then he thought to himself: "I will go and look for old Nestor; maybe he and I will think of something which may help us." So he rose from his bed, and put the sandals on his feet, and wrapped his coat about him, and put the skin of a lion round his shoulders, and took a spear in his hand.

Now it so happened that Menelaus could not sleep that same night, for he knew that it was on his account that the Greeks had come to Troy. So he also rose from his bed, and wrapped the skin of a leopard about his shoulders, and took a spear in his hand, and went to look for his brother. And when he found him, for, as has been said, he also had armed himself, he said: "What seek you? See you the Trojans there? Let us send a spy to find what they are doing, and how many there are of them, for I do not doubt that they are planning something against us. But is there anyone who will dare to do such a thing, for, indeed, it is a great danger."

Agamemnon answered: "It is true, my brother, that we are in great trouble, and need good advice if we are to save the people. Surely Zeus has greatly changed his mind concerning us. There was a time when he favoured us, but now it is of his doing that Hector drives us before him in this fashion. Never did I see a man so manifestly strengthened by Zeus, and yet he is but a man, having neither god for his father, nor goddess for his mother. But go now call the chiefs to counsel, and I will go to Nestor."

So the chiefs were called, and Nestor said: "First let us see whether the watch are sleeping or waking." So they went the round of the wall, and they found the watchmen not sleeping but waking. As a dog that hears the sound of a wild beast in the wood, so they looked towards the plain, thinking to hear the feet of the Trojans. Old Nestor was glad to see them and said: "You do well, my children, lest we become a prey to our enemies."

After this they passed over the trench and sat down in an open place that was clear of dead bodies, for here it was that Hector had turned back from slaying the Greeks when darkness came over the earth. And Nestor rose up and said: "Is there now a man who will go among the Trojans and spy out what it is in their mind to do? Such a one will win great honour to himself, and the King will give him many gifts."

Diomed stood up in his place and said: "I will go, but it is well that I should have someone with me. For to have a companion gives a man courage and comfort; also two wits are better than one."

Many were willing to go with Diomed. And Agamemnon, fearing for his brother Menelaus, offered himself among others and said: "Choose, O Diomed, the man whom you would most desire to have with you; think not of any man's birth or rank; choose only him whom you would best like for a companion."

Then Diomed said: "If I may have my choice, Ulysses shall go with me. He is brave, and he is prudent, and Athene loves him."

Ulysses answered: "Do not praise me too much, nor blame me too much. But let us go, for the night is far spent."

So the two armed themselves. Diomed took a two-edged sword and a shield, and a helmet without a crest, for such is not easy to be seen. Ulysses took a bow with a quiver full of arrows and a sword, and for a helmet a cap of hide, with the white teeth of a wild boar round it. Then they both prayed to Athene that she would help them. That being done, they set out and went through the night, like to two lions, and they trod on dead bodies and arms and blood.

Meanwhile Hector was thinking about the same thing, how that it would be well to find out what the Greeks were doing, and what they were planning for the next day. So he called the chiefs of the Trojans and the allies to a council and said: "Who now will go and spy among the Greeks, and see whether they are keeping a good watch, and find out, if he can overhear them talking together, what they mean to do to-morrow. Such a man shall have a great reward, a chariot, that is to say, with two horses, the best that there is in the whole camp of the Greeks."

Then there stood up a certain Dolon. He was the son of a herald, the only son of his father, but he had five sisters. He was an ill-favoured man, but a swift runner. Dolon said: "I will go, O Hector, but I want a great reward, even the horses of Achilles, for these are the best in the whole camp of the Greeks. Do you lift up your sceptre and swear that you will give me these, and none other."

It was a foolish thing, for who was Dolon that he should have the chariot and horses of the great Achilles? And Hector knew this in his heart; nevertheless he lifted up his sceptre, and swore that he would give to Dolon these horses and none others. Then Dolon armed himself. He took his bow, and a cap of wolf's skin for a helmet, and a sharp spear, and went his way, nor did he try to go quickly, for he did not think that anyone from the camp of the Greeks would be abroad. So Ulysses heard his steps and said to Diomed: "Here comes a man; maybe he is a spy, maybe he is come to spoil the dead bodies. Let him pass by, that we may take him, for we must not suffer him to go back to the city."

So the two lay down among the dead bodies on the plain, and Dolon passed by them, not knowing that they were there. And after he had gone fifty yards or so, then they rose up and ran after him. He heard the noise of their running and stood still, thinking to himself: "Hector has sent men after me; perhaps he wishes me to go back." And this, indeed, he would gladly have done, for he was beginning to be afraid. But when they were but a spear's throw from him, he saw that they were Greeks, and fled. And the two ran after him, as two dogs follow a fawn or a hare, and though he was swift of foot he could not outrun them, nor could they come up to him, but they kept him from turning back to the city. But when they were near the trench, then Diomed called out to the man: "Stop, or I will slay you with my spear." And he threw his spear, not meaning to kill the man, but to frighten him, making it pass over his shoulder, so that it stood in the ground before him. When Dolon saw the spear he stood still, and his teeth chattered with fear. And the two came up to him, breathing hard, for they had been running fast. Then said Dolon, weeping as he spoke: "Do not kill me. My father will pay a great ransom for me, if he hears that you are keeping me at your ships much gold and bronze and iron will he pay for my life."

Ulysses answered: "Be of good cheer. Tell us truly why you were coming through the darkness. Was it to spoil the dead, or did Hector send you to spy out what was going on at the ships, or was it on some private business of your own?"

Dolon answered: "Hector persuaded me to go, promising that he would give me the chariot and horses of Achilles. And

I was to spy out what you had in your minds to do on the morrow and whether you were keeping watch."

Ulysses laughed when the man spoke of the chariot and horses of Achilles. "Truly," he said, "it was a great reward that you deserved. The horses of Achilles are hard to manage, except a man be the son of a god or a goddess. But tell me, where is Hector? and what watch does the Trojan keep?"

Dolon answered: "When I came away from the camp of the Trojans, Hector was holding council with the chiefs close to the tomb of Ilus. As for the watches, there are none set, except in that part of the camp where the Trojans are. As for the allies, they sleep without caring for watches, thinking that the Trojans will do this for them."

Then Ulysses asked again: "Do the allies then sleep among the Trojans or apart?"

Then Dolon told him about the camp, who were in this place and who were in that. "But," he went on, "if you would know where you may best make your way into the camp and not be seen, go to the furthest part upon the left. There are some newcomers, men from Thrace, with Rhesus their king. Never have I seen horses so big and so fine as his. And they are whiter than snow, and swifter than the wind. But now send me to the ships, or, if you cannot do that, having no one to take me, bind me and leave me." But Diomed said: "Think not, Dolon, that we will suffer you to live, though, indeed, you have told us that which we desired to know. For then you would come again to spy out our camp, or, maybe, would fight with us in battle. But if we kill you, then you will trouble us no more."

**DIOMED AND ULYSSES RETURNING WITH THE
SPOILS OF RHESUS**

So they killed him, and stripped him of his arms. These they hung on a tamarisk tree that there was in the place, making a mark with reeds and branches that they might know the place when they came back. Then they went on to the camp of the Trojans, and found the place of which Dolon had told them. There the men of Thrace lay asleep, each man with his arms at his side. And in the midst of the company lay King Rhesus, with his chariot at his side, and the horses tethered to the rail of the chariot. Then Diomed began to slay the men as they slept. He was like a lion in the middle of a fold full of sheep, so fierce and strong was he, and they so helpless. Twelve men he slew, and as he slew them, Ulysses dragged their bodies out of the way, that there might be a clear road for the horses, for horses are wont to start aside when they see a dead body lying in the way. "These maybe," so he thought to himself, "are not used to war." Twelve men did Diomed slay, and King Rhesus the thirteenth, as he lay and panted in his sleep, for he had a bad dream at the very time when Diomed slew him. Meanwhile Ulysses had unbound the horses from the chariot and driven them out of the camp. With his bow he struck them, for he had not thought to take the whip from the chariot. And when he had got the horses clear, then he whistled, for a sign to Diomed that he should come without more delay, for well he knew that Diomed would not easily be satisfied with slaying. And, truly, the man was lingering, doubting whether he might not kill yet more. But Athene whispered in his ear: "Think of your return; maybe some god will rouse the Trojans against you."

And, indeed, Apollo was rousing them. The cousin of King Rhesus awoke and, seeing the place of the horses empty, cried out, calling the King. So all the camp was roused. But Diomed and Ulysses mounted the horses and rode to the camp of the Greeks. Right glad were their comrades to see them and to hear the tale of what they had done.

CHAPTER XVI

THE WOUNDING OF THE CHIEFS

As soon as it was light Agamemnon called the Greeks, and Hector called the Trojans to battle, nor were either unwilling to obey. For a time the fighting was equal, but at noon, at the time when a man who is cutting down trees upon the hills grows weary of his work and longs for food, then the Greeks began to prevail. And the first man to break through the line of the Trojans was King Agamemnon. Never before had the King done such mighty deeds, for he drove the Trojans back to the very walls of the city. Hector himself did not dare to stand up before him, for Iris brought this message to him from Zeus: "So long as Agamemnon fights in the front, do you hold back, for this is the day on which it is his lot to win great honour for himself;

but when he shall be wounded, then do you go forward, and you shall have strength to drive the Greeks before you till they come to the ships, and the sun shall set." So Hector held back, and after a while the King was wounded. There were two sons of Antenor in one chariot, and they came against him. First the King threw his spear at the younger of the two, but missed his aim. Then the Trojan thrust at Agamemnon with his spear, driving it against his breastplate. With all his strength he drove it, but the silver which was in the breastplate turned the spear, so that it bent as if it had been of lead. Then the King caught the spear in his hand, and drove it through the neck of his adversary, so that he fell dead from the chariot. But when the elder brother saw this he also thrust at the King with his spear, nor did he thrust in vain, but he pierced his arm beneath the elbow. But him also did the King slay, wounding him first with his spear and afterwards cutting off his head with his sword. For a time, while the wound was warm, the King still fought, but when it grew cold and stiff, then the pain was greater than he could bear, and he said to his charioteer, "Now carry me back to the ships, for I cannot fight any more."

The next of the chiefs that was wounded was Diomed. Him Paris wounded with an arrow as he was stripping the arms from a Trojan whom he had slain. For Paris hid himself behind the pillar which stood on the tomb of Ilus, and shot his arrows from thence. On the ankle of the right foot did Paris hit him, and when he saw that he had not shot the arrow in vain, he cried out aloud: "I wish that I had wounded you in the loin, bold Diomed, then you would have troubled the men of Troy no more!"

But Diomed answered: "If I could but meet you face to face, you coward, your bow and your arrows would not help you. As for this graze on my foot, I care no more for it than if a woman or a child had struck me. Come near, and I will show you what are the wounds which I make with my spear."

Then he beckoned to Ulysses that he should stand before him while he drew the arrow from his foot. And Ulysses did so. But when he had drawn out the arrow, the pain was so great that he could not stand up, for all the brave words that he had spoken. And he bade his charioteer drive him to the ships.

So Ulysses was left alone. Not one of the chiefs stood by him, for now that King Agamemnon and Diomed had departed, there was great fear upon all the Greeks. And Ulysses said to himself: "Now what shall I do? It would be a shameful thing to fly from these Trojans, though there are many of them, and I am alone; but it would be still worse, if I were to be taken here and slain. Surely it is the doing of Zeus, that this trouble is come upon the Greeks, and who am I that I should fight against Zeus? Yet why do I talk in this way? It is only the coward who draws back; a brave man stands in his place, whether he lives or dies." But while he was thinking these things many Trojans came about him, as dogs come about a wild boar in a wood, and the boar stands at bay, and gnashes his big white teeth. So Ulysses stood, thrusting here and there with his long spear. Five chiefs he slew; but one of the five, before he was slain, wounded him in the side, scraping the flesh from the ribs. Then Ulysses cried out for help; three times he cried, and the third time Menelaus heard him, and called to Ajax.

"O Ajax, I hear the voice of Ulysses, and it sounds like the voice of one who is in great trouble. Maybe the Trojans have surrounded him. Come, let us help him, for it would be a great loss to the Greeks if he were to come to any harm."

Then he led the way to the place from which the voice seemed to come, and Ajax followed him. And when they came to Ulysses, they found it was as Menelaus had said; for the Trojans had beset Ulysses, as the jackals beset a deer with long horns among the hills. The beast cannot fly because the hunter has wounded it with an arrow from his bow, and the wound has become stiff, and he stands at bay. Then a lion comes, and the jackals are scattered in a moment. So the Trojans were scattered when Ajax came. Then Menelaus took Ulysses by the hand, and led him out of the throng, while Ajax drove the Trojans before him.

And now yet another chief was wounded, for Paris from his hiding-place behind the pillar on the tomb of Ilus shot an arrow at Machaon, and wounded him on the right shoulder. And one of the chiefs cried to old Nestor, who was fighting close by: "Quick, Nestor, take Machaon in your chariot, and drive him to the ships, for the life of a physician is worth the lives of many men."

So Nestor took Machaon in his chariot, and touched his horses with the whip, and they galloped to the ships.

Now Hector was fighting on the other side of the plain, and his charioteer said to him: "See how Ajax is driving our people before him. Let us go and stop him." So they went, lashing the horses that they might go the faster, and the chariot rolled over many bodies of men, and the axle and the sides of it were red with blood. Then Zeus put fear into the heart of the great Ajax himself. He would not fly, but he turned round, throwing his great shield over his shoulder, and moved towards the ships slowly, step by step. It was as when an ass breaks into a field and eats the standing corn, and the children of the village beat him with sticks. Their arms are weak, and the sticks are broken on the beast's back, for he is slow in going, nor do they drive him out till he has eaten his fill. So the Trojans thrust at Ajax with their lances. And now he would turn round and face them, and now he would take a step towards the ships.

Now Achilles was standing on the stern of his ship, looking at the battle, and Patroclus stood by him. And when old Nestor passed by taking Machaon to the ships, Achilles said to his friend: "Soon, I think, will the Greeks come and pray me to help them, for they are in great trouble. But go now and see who was this whom Nestor is taking to the ships. His shoulders, I thought, were the shoulders of Machaon, but his face I could not see, for the horses went by very fast."

Then Patroclus ran to do his errand. Meanwhile Nestor took Machaon to his tent. And there the girl that waited on the old man mixed for them a bowl of drink. First she set a table, and laid on it a bronze charger, and on it she put a flask of wine, and a leek, with which to flavour it, and yellow honey, and barley meal. And she fetched from another part of the tent a great bowl with four handles. On each side of the bowl there was a pair of handles, and on each handle there was a dove, wrought in bronze, and the doves seemed to be pecking at each other. A very big bowl it was, and, when it was full, so heavy that a man could scarcely lift it from the table but Nestor, though he was old, could lift it easily. Then the girl poured the wine from the flask into the bowl, and put honey into it, and shredded cheese made of goat's milk, and the leek to flavour it. And when the mess[1] was ready, she bade them drink. So they drank, and talked together.

But while they talked, Patroclus stood in the door of the tent. And Nestor went to him, and took him by the hand, and said: "Come now and sit down with us, and drink from the bowl." But Patroclus would not. "Stay me not," he said; "I came to see who it was whom you have brought wounded out of the battle. And now I see that it is Machaon. Therefore I will go back without delay, for you know what kind of man is Achilles, how he quickly grows angry and is ready to blame."

Then said Nestor: "What does Achilles care about the Greeks? Why does he ask who are wounded? O Patroclus, do you remember the day when Ulysses and I came to the house of Peleus? Your father was there, and we feasted in the hall; and when the feast was finished, then we told Peleus why we had come, how we were gathering the chiefs of Greece to go and fight against Troy. And you and Achilles were eager to go. And the old men gave you much advice. Old Peleus said to Achilles: 'You must always be the very first in the battle.' But to you your father said: 'Achilles is of nobler birth than you, and he is stronger by far. But you are older, and years give wisdom. Therefore it will be your part to give him good counsel when there is need.' Why then do you not advise him to help us? And if he is still resolved not to go forth to the

---

[1] Editor's Note: Archaic use, but a term still used in the military

battle, then let him send you forth, and his people with you, and let him lend you his armour to wear. Then the Trojans will think that Achilles himself has come back to the battle, and they will be afraid, and we shall have a breathing space."

Then Patroclus turned and ran back to the tent of Achilles.

CHAPTER XVII

THE BATTLE AT THE WALL

Now by this time the Trojans were close upon the trench but there they stood, for the horses were afraid, the trench being deep, and having great stakes set in it. Then Polydamas, who was one of the wisest of the Trojans, said to Hector: "This is but a mad thing, O Hector, to try to cross the trench in our chariots, for it is wide, and has many stakes set in it. Look too at this: how will it be when we have crossed it? If, indeed, it is the pleasure of Zeus that the Greeks should perish utterly—well; but if, as has come to pass before, not once only, the Greeks take heart and turn upon us and drive us back, what shall we do? Nay; let us leave our chariots here, and if need be, we can come back and find them waiting for us. But we will go on foot against the wall."

So they jumped down from their chariots and went against the walls on foot. In five companies they went. The first, which was the largest and had in it the bravest of the Trojans, Hector himself led. And the next was commanded by Paris. The third was led by Helenus the prophet, and with him was Deïphobus, who also was a son of King Priam; and Asius, one of the allies, who was King of Arisbe. Of the fourth Aeneas was the leader, and of the fifth Sarpedon of Lycia with Glaucus and others from among the allies. They stood closely to each other, holding shield by shield, and so they went against the Greeks. All of them, also, left their chariots on this side of the trench, all except King Asius only. But he drove his chariot to a place where there was a road over the trench, and on the other side a gate. And this gate chanced to be open, for the keepers had set it open, so that any of the Greeks who were flying from the Trojans might find refuge inside it. When the keepers, who were two mighty men of valour, saw Asius and his company coming, they went forward and stood in front of the gate, for they had not time to shut it. There they stood, just as two wild boars might stand at bay against a crowd of men and dogs. And all the while the men who stood on the wall never ceased to throw down heavy stones on the Trojans. The stones fell as fast as the flakes of snow fall on a winter's day, and the helmets and shields of the Trojans rang out as the stones crashed upon them. Many fell to the ground, and King Asius, for all his fury, could not make his way through the gate.

At another of the gates, where Hector was leading his company, there was seen a very strange thing in the skies. An eagle had caught a great snake, and was carrying it in

**POLYDAMAS ADVISING HECTOR TO RETIRE
FROM THE TRENCH**

his claws to give to its young ones for food. But the snake fought fiercely for its life, and writhed itself about till it bit the bird upon the breast. And when the eagle felt that it had been bitten, it dropped the snake into the middle of the two armies, and flew away with a loud cry. Then Polydamas, who was a wise man, and knew the meaning of all such signs, said to Hector: "O Hector, it will be well for us not to follow the Greeks to their ships. For this strange thing which we have just seen in the sky is a sign to us. The eagle signifies the Trojans, and the snake signifies the Greeks. Now, as the eagle caught the snake but could not hold it, so we have prevailed over the Greeks, but shall not be able to conquer them altogether. And as the snake turned upon the bird and bit it, so will the Greeks turn upon us and do us great damage, so that we shall be driven back from the ships, and leave many of our comrades dead behind us."

But Hector was angry to hear such words, and said: "This is bad advice that you give me. Surely the gods have changed your wisdom into foolishness. Would you have me forget the commandment of Zeus, when he bade me follow the Greeks even to their ships, and take heed to birds, and do one thing or another because they fly this way or that? Little do I care whether they fly east or west or are seen on the right hand or on the left. Surely there is but one sign for a brave man, that he be fighting for his fatherland. Take heed, therefore, to yourself. Truly if you hold back from the war, or cause any other man to hold back, I will smite you with my spear."

Then he sprang forward, and the Trojans followed him with a great shout. And Zeus sent down from Mount Ida a great wind, and the wind carried the dust of the plain straight into the faces of the Greeks, troubling them not a little. But when the Trojans sought to drag down the battlements which were on the wall and to pull up the stakes which had been set to strengthen it, they could not, for the building was strong, and the Greeks stood firm in their place, with shield joining to shield, and fought for the wall.

After a while Sarpedon the Lycian came to the front, for Zeus put it into his heart so to do, that he might win great glory for himself. He came holding his shield before him and with a long spear in either hand. Just as a lion, when he is mad with hunger, goes against a stable in which oxen are kept, or against a sheepfold, and does not care though it is guarded by many men and dogs, so did Sarpedon go against the wall. And he spoke to Glaucus, his kinsman, saying:

"Tell me, Glaucus, why it is that our people at home honour us with the chief places at feasts, and with fat portions of flesh, and with wine of the best, and that they have set apart for us a great domain of orchard and of plough-land by the banks of the Xanthus. Surely it is that we may fight in the front rank, and show to others how they should behave in the battle. For so someone who may see us will say, 'Of a truth these are honourable men, these princes of Lycia, and not without good right do they eat the fat and drink the sweet, for they are always to be seen fighting in the front.' Maybe, if we could hope to live forever, and to escape from old age and death, I would not either fight myself in the front or bid you do so; but now, seeing that there are ten thousand chances of death about us, let us see whether we may not win glory from another, or haply another may win it from us."

When he had so spoken he leapt forward, and Glaucus went with him, and all the host of the Lycians followed close behind. Then the keeper of the gate—he was a man of Athens—was struck with great fear and looked about for help. All along the wall he looked, and he saw Ajax the Greater and Ajax the Less, and Teucer, for the hurt which Hector had given him was now healed. He would have shouted to them, but the din of arms, and the ringing of shields and helmets and the battering at the gates, would have drowned his voice. So he called a herald, and said: "Run now, and call Ajax hither—both the Greater and the Less, if it may be—for the danger is very great, and the chiefs of the Lycians press us hard. And if there is trouble there also, then let Ajax the Greater come at the least and Teucer with him, bringing his bow." So the herald ran with the message, and when Ajax the Greater heard it, he said to the other Ajax: "Stand here and keep off the enemy; and I will go yonder, and come again when I have done my work."

So Ajax, and Teucer his brother, ran as quickly as they could to the gate, and just as they got to it the Lycians came against it with a great rush, as if it had been a storm of wind and rain. But still the Greeks stood firm, and Ajax slew one of the Lycian chiefs and Teucer wounded Glaucus on the shoulder. Quietly he jumped down from the wall, for he did not wish that anyone should see that he was wounded. But Sarpedon saw it and was sorry, because he was his kinsman and also a great help in the battle. Nevertheless he pressed on as bravely as before. First he slew one of the Greeks upon the wall, and then he laid hold of one of the battlements with his two hands and pulled it down, and a part of the wall with it. Thus there was a way made by which men might enter the camp. But Ajax and his brother stopped the Lycians for a time, aiming at Sarpedon, both of them together. Teucer struck at him with his spear, for the bow he could not use when the enemy was so near, and smote the strap of his shield, but did him no harm; Ajax drove his spear through the shield and pushed him back, so that he was forced to leap from the wall to the ground. But his courage was not one whit abated. He cried out: "Help me now, ye men of Lycia. It is hard for me, however great my strength, to do this work alone, pulling down the wall and making a way for you to the ships." And all his people, when they heard his voice, came rushing up in a great crowd. But the Greeks, on the other hand, strengthened their line, others coming to the place where they saw the need to be greatest, for indeed it was a matter of life and death. For a long time they fought with equal strength, for the Lycians could not break down the wall and make a way to the ships, and the Greeks could not drive the Lycians back.

But at the last Zeus gave the glory to Hector. Once again he sprang to the front, crying: "Now follow me, men of Troy, and we will burn the ships." In front of the gate there lay a great stone, broad at the bottom and sharp at the top. Scarcely could two men, the strongest that there are in these days, lift it on to a wagon; but Hector took it up as easily as a shepherd carries in one hand the fleece of a sheep. Now there were two folding doors in the middle of the gate, by which a man might enter without opening the gate. These doors were fastened by a bolt and a key. Then Hector lifted the great stone above his head, holding it with both his hands, and he put his feet apart, that his aim might be the surer and stronger, and threw it with all his might at the doors. With a mighty crash did it come against them, and the bolts could not hold against it, and the hinges were broken, and the doors flew back. Then Hector leapt into the open space, holding a spear in either hand, and his eyes flashed with fire. And the Trojans followed him, some entering by the gate and some climbing over the wall.

CHAPTER XVIII

THE BATTLE AT THE SHIPS

Now Poseidon, the god of the sea, loved the Greeks, and when he saw from a distant mountain where he sat how they fled before the Trojans, he was greatly troubled; and he said to himself: "Now I will help these men." It happened, also, that Zeus had turned his eyes from the battle, thinking that none of the gods would do the thing which he had forbidden, that is, bring help to the Greeks. So Poseidon left the mountain where he sat, and came to his palace under the sea. There he harnessed his horses to his chariot, and he passed over the waves, while the great beasts of the sea, whales and porpoises and the like, gambolled round him as he went, because they knew that he was their king. And when he came to the land of Troy, he left his chariot in a cave, and went on foot into the camp of the

Greeks, having made himself like to Calchas the herald. And he came to the place where Ajax the Greater and the other Ajax were standing, and said to them: "Stir yourselves, for it is for you, who are stronger than other men, to save the people. I do not fear for the rest of the wall, but only for the place where Hector is fighting. Go then and keep him back, and may some god give you strength and courage."

And as he spoke he touched them with his staff and filled them with fresh courage, and gave new strength to their hands and to their feet. And when he had done this, he passed out of their sight, as quickly as a hawk flies when he drops from a cliff, chasing a bird. Then the Lesser Ajax perceived that he was not Calchas the herald but a god; and he said to the other Ajax: "This is a god who sends us to the battle. I knew him as he went away and truly I feel my heart in me eager for the fight." And Ajax the Greater answered: "So it is with me also. I am all on fire for the battle. I would go against this Hector, even should I go alone." Meanwhile Poseidon went through the army, stirring up the other chiefs in the same way. But still the Trojans came on, even fiercer than before. Then Teucer slew a famous chief, Imbrius by name, driving his spear point under the man's ear. Like to some tall poplar by a river-side which a woodman cuts down with his axe of bronze, so did Imbrius fall. Then Hector cast his spear at Teucer. Him he missed, but he struck the comrade who was standing next to him. And Hector, as the man lay upon the ground, seized his helmet, and would have dragged the body among his own people. But Ajax the Greater thrust with his spear, and struck the boss of Hector's shield so strongly that he was driven backward and loosed his hold of the helmet, and the Greeks carried the man to the ships. Next there was slain a chief from the land of Caria who had come to Troy, desiring to have Cassandra, daughter of King Priam, for his wife. Loudly had he boasted, saying that he would drive the Greeks to the ships; and the King had promised him his daughter. But now he was slain. And the King of the Cretans, when he saw him lie dead, cried: "Truly this was a great thing which you promised to King Priam, so that he might give you his daughter. You should have come rather to us, and Agamemnon would have given you the fairest of his daughters, bringing her from Argos, that she might be married to you, if only you would take for us this city of Troy. But come now with me to the ships, that we may treat with you about this matter. Verily you will find that we Greeks are men of an open hand." Thus did the King speak, mocking the dead.

King Asius heard these words and was full of anger, and came at the Prince of Crete, lifting his spear to throw it. He was on foot, and his chariot followed close after him. But before he could cast the spear the Prince of Crete smote him full on the breast, and he fell as an oak or a pine tree falls before the axes of the wood-cutters on the hills. And when the driver of the chariot saw his master fall he was struck with fear, not knowing what to do. Then Antilochus, who was the eldest son of old Nestor, struck him down with his spear, and jumped on to the chariot, and took it and the horses for his own. Many other of the Trojans did the Greeks slay, and many they wounded. Even the mighty Hector himself was struck down for a time. He cast his spear at the great Ajax but hurt him not, for the point was turned by the armour, so thick it was and strong. And when he saw that he had cast the spear in vain, then he turned, and sought to go back to the ranks of his comrades; but, as he went, Ajax took up from the ground a great stone, one of many that lay there, and served as props for the ships, and cast it at Hector, smiting him above the rim of his shield on the neck. He fell as an oak falls when the lightning has struck it, and the Greeks, when they saw him fall, rushed with a great cry, and would have caught hold of his body and dragged it away. But this the Trojans did not suffer, for many of the bravest of them stood before him, covering him with their shields. And when they had driven back the Greeks a space, they lifted him from the ground, and carried him to the river and poured water upon him, After a while he sat up, and then his spirit left him again, for it was a grievous blow which Ajax had dealt him. But when the Greeks saw that Hector had been carried out of the battle, they took fresh courage and charged the Trojans, and drove them back even beyond the walls and the trench. And when the Trojans came to the place where they had left their chariots and horses, they stood pale and trembling, not knowing what to do.

But now Zeus turned his eyes again to the land of Troy. Very angry was he when he saw what had happened, how the Trojans fled from the Greeks, and Hector lay upon the plain, like to one that has fallen in battle, and his friends stood round him in great fear lest he had been wounded to the death. So he said to Hera: "Is this then your doing, rebellious one? Tell me now the truth, or it will be the worse for you." And Hera answered: "Nay, this is not my doing. It is Poseidon who gives to the Greeks strength and courage." Then said Zeus to Iris the messenger: "Go now to Poseidon and

**AJAX DEFENDING THE GREEK SHIPS AGAINST
THE TROJANS**

tell him that it is my will that he is not to meddle with these things anymore. Let him go back to the sea, for there he is master; but the things that happen on the earth, these belong to me. And when you have given this message to Poseidon, then go to Apollo and bid him go to Hector where he lies like a dead man on the plain, and put new life and courage into him, and send him back with new strength to the battle."

So Iris went on her errand. First she came to Poseidon, and gave him the message of Zeus. He was very angry when he heard it, and said: "Am I not his equal in honour? By what right does he bid me do this thing and cease from doing that? We were three brothers, sons of Old Time, and to me was given the dominion of the sea, and to Pluto the dwellings of the dead, and to Zeus to reign over the heaven and the earth."

But Iris answered: "O Poseidon, is it well to speak thus of Zeus? Do you not know how the eldest born is ever the strongest?" And Poseidon answered: "These are words of wisdom, O Iris, yet truly, if Zeus is minded to save this city of Troy, there will be enmity without ceasing between him and me." Then went Iris to Apollo and gave him the message of Zeus. So Apollo hastened to Hector where he sat by the river-side, for already his strength had begun to come back to him. And Apollo said to him: "Why is this, O Hector? Why do you sit here and take no part in the battle?"

Hector answered: "Is this a god that speaks to me? Did you not see how Ajax struck me down with a great stone, so that I could not fight any more? Truly, I thought that I had gone down to the place of the dead." Apollo said: "Take courage, my friend. I am Apollo of the Golden Sword, and Zeus has sent me to stand by you and to help you. Come now, call the Trojans together again, and go before them, and lead them to the ships, and I will be with you and make the way easy for you." Then Hector stood up, and his strength came back to him as it had been before, and he called to the Trojans and went before them. The Greeks wondered when they saw him, for they thought that he had been wounded to death. They were like men who hunt a stag or a wild goat and find a lion. Nevertheless they kept up their courage, and stood close together with their faces towards the enemy but though the chiefs stood firm, most of the Greeks turned their backs and fled. And Hector still came on and Apollo went before him, having a cloud of fire round his shoulders, and holding the great shield of Zeus in his hand. Many of the Greeks were slain that day. And now the Trojans came again to the trench and crossed it, and neither the wall nor the gates stopped them, and they came as far as the ships, Hector being first of all. And close behind Hector was a chief who carried a torch in his hand, with which to set fire to a ship. Him Ajax smote on the breast with his sword and killed him. And Hector, when he saw it, cast his spear at Ajax. Him he missed, but he killed the comrade who was standing close by him. Then Ajax called to Teucer: "Where is your bow and your arrows? Shoot!" So Teucer shot. With the first arrow he slew a Trojan; but when he laid another arrow upon the string and aimed it at Hector, the string broke, and the arrow went far astray. When Teucer saw this he cried out: "Surely the gods are against us; see how the string of my bow is broken, and yet it was new this very day." And Ajax said to him: "Let your bow be, if the gods will not have you use it. Take your spear and fight. Truly, if the men of Troy prevail over us, yet they shall not take our ships for nothing." So Teucer threw away his bow, and took up spear and shield. When Hector saw it, he cried: "Come on, men of Troy, for Zeus is with us, and they whom Zeus favours are strong, and they whom he favours not are weak. See now how he has broken the bow of Teucer, the great archer. Come on, therefore, for the gods give us victory. And even if a man die, it is a noble thing to die fighting for his country. His wife and children shall dwell in peace, and he himself shall be famous forever."

Thus did Hector urge on his people to the battle; and Ajax, on the other hand, called to the Greeks and bade them quit themselves like men. Many chiefs fell on either side, but still the Trojans prevailed more and more, and the Greeks fell back before them. And now Hector laid hold on one of the ships. Well did he know it, for it was the very first that had touched the Trojan shore, and he had slain the chief whose ship it was with his own hand as he was leaping to the shore. There the battle grew fiercer and fiercer; none fought with arrows or javelins, but close, man to man, with swords and battle-axes and spears, thrusting at each other. And Hector cried: "Bring me fire that we may burn the ships of these robbers, for Zeus has given us the victory to-day." And the Trojans came on more fiercely than before, so that Ajax himself was forced to give way, so much did the Trojans press him. For at first he stood on the stern deck, the ships being drawn up with the stern to the land and the forepart to the sea, and then being driven from the deck, in the middle of the ships, among the benches of the rowers. But still he fought bravely, thrusting at anyone who came near to set fire to the ship. And he cried to the Greeks with a terrible voice, saying: "Now must you quit yourselves as men, O Greeks! Have you any to help you if you are conquered now? Have you any walls behind which you may seek for shelter? There is no city here with a wall and towers and battlements behind which you may hide yourselves. You are in the plain of Troy, and the sea is close behind us, and we are far from our own country. All our hope, therefore, is in courage, for there is no one to save if you will not save yourselves."

So did Ajax speak to the Greeks, and still as he spoke he thrust at the Trojans with his spear.

CHAPTER XIX

THE DEEDS AND DEATH OF PATROCLUS

Patroclus stood by Achilles, weeping bitterly. And Achilles said to him: "What is the matter, Patroclus, that you weep? You are like a girl-child that runs along by her mother's side, and holds her gown and cries till she takes her up in her arms. Have you heard bad news from Phthia? Yet your father still lives, I know, and so does the old man Peleus. Or are you weeping for the Greeks because they perish for their folly, or, maybe, for the folly of their King?"

Then Patroclus answered: "Be not angry with me, great Achilles. The Greeks are in great trouble, for all the bravest of their chiefs are wounded, and yet you still keep your anger, and will not help them. They say that Peleus was your father and Thetis your mother. Yet I should say, so hard are you, that a rock was your father and your mother the sea. If you will not go forth to the battle because you have had some warning from the gods, then let me go, and let your people, the Myrmidons, go with me. And let me put on your armour; the Trojans will think that you have come back to the battle, and the Greeks will have a breathing space."

So Patroclus spoke, entreating Achilles, but he did not know that it was for his own death that he asked. And Achilles answered: "It is no warning that I heed, and that keeps me back from the battle. Such things trouble me not. But these men were not ashamed to stand by when their King took away from me the prize which I had won with my own hands. But let the past be past. I said that I would not fight again till the Trojans should bring the fire near to my own ships. But now, for I see that the people are in great need, you may put on my armour, and lead my people to the fight. And, indeed, it is time to give help, for I see that the Trojans are gathered about the ships, and that the Greeks have scarce standing ground between their enemies and the sea. And I do not see anywhere either Diomed with his spear, nor King Agamemnon; only I hear the voice of Hector, as he calls his people to the battle. Go, therefore, Patroclus, and keep the fire from the ships. But when you have done this, come back and fight no more with the Trojans, for it is my business to conquer them, and you must not take my glory from me. And mind this also: when you feel the joy of battle in your heart, be not over-bold, go not near to the wall of Troy, lest one of the gods meet you and harm you. For these gods love the Trojans, and especially the great archer Apollo with his deadly bow."

**SLEEP AND DEATH CONVEYING THE BODY
OF SARPEDON TO LYCIA**

So these two talked together in the tent. But at the ships Ajax could hold out no longer. For the javelins came thick upon him and clattered on his helmet and his breastplate, and his shoulder was weary with the weight of his great shield. Heavily and hard did he breathe, and the great drops of sweat fell upon the ground. Then, at the last, Hector came near and struck at him with his sword. Him he did not hit, but he cut off the head of his spear. Great fear came on Ajax and he gave way, and the Trojans put torches to the ship's stern, and a great flame rose up into the air. When Achilles saw the flames, he struck his thigh with his hand and said: "Make haste, Patroclus, for I see the fire rising up from the ships."

Then Patroclus put on the armour—breastplate and shield and helmet—and bound the sword on his shoulder, and took a great spear in his hand. But the great Pelian spear he did not take, for that no man could wield but Achilles only. Then the charioteer yoked the horses to the chariot. Two of the horses, Bayard and Piebald, were immortal, but the third was of a mortal breed. And while he did this, Achilles called the Myrmidons to battle. Fifty ships he had brought to Troy, and fifty men in each. And when they were assembled he said: "Forget not, ye Myrmidons, what you said when first I kept you back from the battle, how angry you were, and how you blamed me, complaining that I kept you back against your will. Now you have the thing that you desired."

So the in close array, helmet to helmet and shield to shield, close together as are the stones which a builder builds into a wall. Patroclus went before them in the chariot of Achilles, with the charioteer by his side. And as they went, Achilles went to the chest which stood in his tent, and opened it, and took from it a great cup which Thetis his mother had given him. No man drank out of that cup but Achilles only. Nor did he pour libations out of it to any of the gods but to Zeus only. First he cleansed the cup with sulphur and then with water from the spring. After this he filled it with wine, and standing in the space before the tent he poured out from it to Zeus, saying: "O Zeus, this day I send my dear comrade to the battle. Be thou with him; make him strong and bold, and give him glory, and bring him home safe to the ships, and my people with him."

So he prayed; and Father Zeus heard his prayer: part he granted, but part he denied.

Meanwhile Patroclus with the Myrmidons had come to the place where the battle was so hot, namely, the ship to which Hector had put the torch and set it on fire. And when the Trojans saw him and the armour which he wore, they thought that it had been Achilles, who had put away his anger, and had come forth again to the battle. Nor was it long before they turned to flee. So the battle rolled back again to the trench, and many chariots of the Trojans were broken, for when they crossed it for the second time they took their chariots with them but the horses of Achilles sprang across it in their stride, so nimble were they and so strong. And great was the fear of the Trojans; even the great Hector fled. The heart of Patroclus was set upon slaying him, for he had forgotten the command which Achilles had laid upon him, that when he had saved the ships from the fire he should not fight any more. But though he followed hard after him, he could not overtake him, so swift were the Trojan horses. Then he left following him and turned back, and caused the chariot to be driven backwards and forwards, so that he might slay the Trojans as they sought to fly to the city.

But there were some among the Trojans and their allies who would not flee. Among these was Sarpedon the Lycian; and he, when he saw his people flying before Patroclus, cried aloud to them: "Stand now and be of good courage: I myself will try this great warrior and see what he can do." So he leapt down from his chariot, and Patroclus also leapt down from his, and the two rushed at each other, fierce and swift as two eagles. Sarpedon carried a spear in either hand, and he threw both of them together. With the one he wounded to the death one of the horses of Achilles, that which was of a mortal strain, but the other missed its aim, flying over the left shoulder of Patroclus. But the spear of Patroclus missed not its aim. Full on the heart of Sarpedon it fell, and broke through his armour, and bore him to the earth. He fell, as a pine or a poplar falls on the hills before the woodman's axe. And as he fell, he called to Glaucus his kinsman: "Now show yourself a man, O Glaucus; suffer not the Greeks to spoil me of my arms." And when he had said so much, he died. Now Glaucus was still troubled by the wound which Teucer the archer had given him. But when he heard the voice of Sarpedon he prayed to Apollo, saying: "Give me now strength that I may save the body of my kinsman from the hands of the Greeks." And Apollo heard him and made him whole of his wound. Then he called first to the Lycians, saying, "Fight for the body of your king," and next to the Trojans, that they should honour the man who had come from his own land to help them, and lastly to Hector himself, who had now returned to the battle. "Little care you, O Hector," he said, "for your allies. Lo! Sarpedon is dead, slain by Patroclus. Will you suffer the Myrmidons to carry off his body and do dishonour to it?"

Hector was much troubled by these words, and so were all the men of Troy, for among the allies there was none braver than Sarpedon. So they charged and drove back the Greeks from the body and the Greeks charged again in their turn. No one would have known the great Sarpedon as he lay in the middle of the tumult, so covered was he with dust and blood. But at the last the Greeks drove back the Trojans from the body, and stripped it of its arms but the body itself they harmed not. For at the bidding of Zeus, Apollo came down and carried it out of the tumult, and gave it to Sleep and Death that they should carry it to the land of Lycia. Then again Patroclus forgot the commands of Achilles, for he thought in his heart, "Now shall I take the city of Troy," for, when he had driven the Trojans up to the very gates, he himself climbed on to an angle of the wall. Three times did he climb upon it, and three times did Apollo push him back, laying his hand upon the boss of his shield. And when Patroclus climbed for the fourth time, then Apollo cried to him in a dreadful voice: "Go back, Patroclus; it is not for you to take the great city of Troy, no, nor even for Achilles, who is a far better man than you." Then Patroclus went back, for he feared the anger of the god. But though he thought no more of taking the city, he raged no less against the Trojans. Then did Apollo put it into the heart of Hector to go against the man. So Hector said to his charioteer: "We will see whether we cannot drive back this Patroclus, for it must be he;

Achilles he is not, though he wears his armour." When Patroclus saw them coming he took a great stone from the ground, and cast it at the pair. The stone struck the charioteer full on the helmet. And as the man fell head foremost from the chariot, Patroclus laughed aloud, and said: "See now, how nimble is this man! See how well he dives! He might get many oysters from the bottom of the sea, diving from the deck of a ship, even though it should be a stormy day. Who would have thought that there would be such skilful divers in Troy?"

Three times did Patroclus charge into the ranks of the Trojans, and each time he slew nine warriors. But when he charged the fourth time, then, for the hour of his doom was come, Apollo stood behind him, and gave him a great blow on his neck, so that he could not see out of his eyes. And the helmet fell from his head, so that the plumes were soiled with the dust. Never before had it touched the ground, from the first day when Achilles wore it. The spear also which he carried in his hand was broken, and the shield fell from his arm, and the breastplate on his body was loosened. Then, as he stood without defence and confused, one of the Trojans wounded him in the back with his spear. And when he tried to hide himself behind his comrades, for the wound was not mortal, Hector thrust at him with his spear, and hit him above the hip, and he fell to the ground. And when the Greeks saw him fall they sent up a dreadful cry. Then Hector stood over him, and said: "Did you think, Patroclus, that you would take our city, and slay us with the sword, and carry away our wives and daughters in your ships? This you will not do, for, lo! I have overcome you with my spear, and the fowls of the air shall eat your flesh. And the great Achilles cannot help you at all. Did he not say to you, 'Strip the fellow's shirt from his back and bring it to me'? and you, in your folly, thought that you would do it."

Patroclus answered: "You boast too much, O Hector. It is not by your hand that I am overcome it has been Apollo who has brought me to my death. Had twenty such as you are come against me, truly I had slain them all. And mark you this: death is very near to you, for the great Achilles will slay you."

Then said Hector: "Why do you prophesy my death? Who has shown you the things to come? Maybe, as I have slain you, so shall I also slay the great Achilles." So Hector spoke, but Patroclus was dead already. Then he drew the spear from the wound, and went after the charioteer of Achilles, hoping to slay him and to take the chariot for spoil, but the horses were so swift that he could not come up with them.

CHAPTER XX

THE ROUSING OF ACHILLES

Very fierce was the fight for the body of Patroclus, and many warriors fell both on this side and on that; and the first to be killed was the man who had wounded him in the back for when he came near to strip the dead man of his arms, King Menelaus thrust at him with his spear and slew him. He slew him, but he could not strip off his arms, because Hector came and stood over the body, and Menelaus did not dare to stand up against him, knowing that he was not a match for him in fighting. Then Hector spoiled the body of Patroclus of the arms which the great Achilles had given him to wear. But when he laid hold of the body, and began to drag it away to the ranks of the Trojans, the Greater Ajax came forward, and put his big shield before it. As a lioness stands before its cubs and will not suffer the hunter to take them, so did Ajax stand before the body of Patroclus and defend it from the Trojans. And Hector drew back when he saw him. Then Glaucus the Lycian spoke to him in great anger: "Are you not ashamed, O Hector, that you dare not stand before Ajax? How will you and the other Trojans save your city? Truly your allies will not fight any more for you, for though they help you much, yet you help them but little. Did not Sarpedon fall fighting for you, and yet you left him to be a prey to the dogs? And now, had you only stood up against this Ajax, and dragged away the body of Patroclus, we might have made an exchange, giving him and his arms, and receiving Sarpedon from the Greeks. But this may not be, because you are afraid of Ajax, and flee before him when he comes to meet you."

Hector answered: "I am not afraid of Ajax, nor of any man. But this I know, that Zeus gives victory now to one and now to another; this only do I fear, and this only, to go against the will of Zeus. But wait here, and see whether or no I am a coward."

Now he had sent the armour of Patroclus to the city; but when he heard Glaucus speak in this manner, he ran after the men who were carrying it and overtook them, and stripped off his own armour, and put on the armour of Achilles. And when Zeus saw him do this thing he was angry, and said to himself, "These arms will cost Hector dear." Nevertheless, when he came back to the battle, all men were astonished, for he seemed like to the great Achilles himself. Then the Trojans took heart again, and charged all together, and the battle grew fiercer and fiercer. For the Greeks said to themselves: "It were better that the earth should open her

THE FIGHT FOR THE BODY OF PATROCLUS

mouth and swallow us up alive than that we should let the Trojans carry off the body of Patroclus." And the Trojans said to themselves: "Now if we must all be slain fighting for the body of this man, be it so; but we will not yield." Now while they fought the horses of Achilles stood apart from the battle, and the tears rushed down from their eyes, for they loved Patroclus, and they knew that he was dead. Still they stood in the same place; they would not enter into the battle, neither would they turn back to the ships. And the charioteer could not move them with the lash, or with threats, or with gentle words. As a pillar stands by the grave of some dead man, so they stood their heads drooped to the ground, and the tears trickled down from their eyes, and their long manes were trailed in the dust.

When Zeus saw them he pitied them in his heart. And he said: "It was not well that I gave you, immortal as you are, to a mortal man, for of all things that live and move upon the earth, surely man is the most miserable. But Hector shall not have you. It is enough for him, yea, it is too much that he should have the arms of Achilles."

Then the horses moved from their place, and obeyed their driver as before; and Hector could not take them, though he greatly desired so to do.

All this time the battle raged yet more and more fiercely about the body of Patroclus. At the last, when the Greeks were growing weary, and the Trojans pressed them more and more, Ajax said to Menelaus, for these two had borne themselves more bravely in the battle than all the others: "See now if you can find Antilochus, Nestor's son, and bid him run and carry the news to Achilles that Patroclus is dead, and that the Greeks and Trojans are fighting for his body." So Menelaus went, and found Antilochus on the left side of the battle. And he said to him: "I have bad news for you. You see that the Trojans prevail in the battle today. And now Patroclus lies dead. Run, therefore, to Achilles and tell him maybe he can yet save the body; as for the arms, Hector has them."

Antilochus was greatly troubled to hear the news, his eyes filled with tears, and he could not speak for grief. But he gave heed to the words of Menelaus, and ran to tell Achilles what had happened.

And Menelaus went back to Ajax, where he had left him standing close by the body of Patroclus. And he said to him: "I have found Antilochus, and he is carrying the news to Achilles. Yet I doubt whether he will come to the battle, however great his anger may be and his grief, for he has no armour to cover him. Let us think, therefore, how we may best save the body of Patroclus from the Trojans."

Ajax said: "Do you and Meriones run forward and lift up the body and carry it away." So Menelaus and Meriones ran forward and lifted up the body. But when they would have carried it away, then the Trojans ran fiercely at them. So the battle raged neither could the Greeks save the body, nor could the Trojans carry it away. Meanwhile Antilochus came to Achilles where he sat by the door of his tent. With a great fear in his heart he sat, for he saw that the Greeks fled and the Trojans pursued after them. Then said Nestor's son: "I bring bad news. Patroclus is dead, and Hector has his arms, but the Greeks and Trojans are fighting for his body."

Then Achilles threw himself upon the ground, and took the dust in his hands, and poured it on his head, and tore his hair. And all the women wailed aloud. And Antilochus sat weeping; but while he wept he held the hands of Achilles, for he was afraid that in his anger he would do himself a mischief. But his mother heard his cry, where she sat in the depths of the sea, and came to him and laid her hand upon his head, and said: "Why do you weep, my son? Tell me; hide not the matter from me." Achilles answered: "All that you asked from Zeus, and that he promised to do, he has done: but what is the good? The man whom I loved above all others is dead, and Hector has my arms, for Patroclus was wearing them. As for me, I do not wish to live except to avenge myself upon him."

Then said Thetis: "My son, do not speak so: do you not know that when Hector dies, the hour is near when you also must die?"

Then Achilles cried in great anger: "I would that I could die this hour, for I sent my friend to his death; and I, who am better in battle than all the Greeks, could not help him. Cursed be the anger that sets men to strive[1] with one another, as it made me strive with King Agamemnon. And as for my fate—what matters it? Let it come when it may, so that I may first have vengeance on Hector. Seek not, therefore, my mother, to keep me back from the battle."

---

[1] Editor's Note: Archaic use of "strive": to struggle or compete with one another. From Old French "estriver": to quarrel, c. 1200. To Middle English "striven": to compete or endeavor.

Thetis answered: "Be it so, my son: only you cannot go without arms, and these Hector has. But to-morrow I will go to Hephaestus, that he may make new arms for you."

But while they talked, the Trojans pressed the Greeks still more and more, so that Ajax himself could no longer stand against them. Then truly they would have taken the body of Patroclus, had not Zeus sent Iris to Achilles with this message: "Rouse yourself, son of Peleus, or, surely, Patroclus will be a prey to the dogs of Troy." But Achilles said: "How shall I go? For I have no arms, nor do I know of any one whose arms I could wear. I might shift with the shield of great Ajax; but this he is carrying, as is his custom, in the front of the battle."

Then said Iris: "Go only to the trench and show yourself, for the Trojans will be swift and draw back, and the Greeks will have a breathing space."

So Achilles ran to the trench. And Athene put her great shield about his shoulders, and set as it were a circle of gold about his head, so that it shone like to a flame of fire. To the trench he went, but he obeyed the word of his mother, and did not mix in the battle. Only he shouted aloud, and his voice was as the voice of a trumpet. It was a terrible sound to hear, and the hearts of the men of Troy were filled with fear. The very horses were frightened, and started aside, so that the chariots clashed together. Three times did Achilles shout across the trench, and three times did the Trojans fall back. Twelve chiefs perished that hour; some were wounded by their own spears, and some were trodden down by their own horses; for the whole army was overcome with fear, from the front ranks to the hindermost. Then the Greeks took up the body of Patroclus from the place where it lay, and put it on the bier,[1] and carried it to the tent of Achilles, and Achilles himself walked by its side weeping. This had been a sad day, and to bring it sooner to an end Hera commanded the sun to set before his time. So did the Greeks rest from their labours.

On the other side of the field, the Trojans held an assembly. And one of the elders stood up and said: "Let us not wait here for the morning. It was well for us to fight at the ships so long as Achilles was angry with King Agamemnon. But now this has ceased to be. To-morrow will he come back to the battle, the fiercer on account of his great grief, Patroclus being slain. Surely it will be an evil day for us, if we wait his coming. Let us go back to the city, for its walls are high and its gates are strong, and the man who seeks to pass them will perish."

But Hector said: "This is bad counsel. Shall we shut up ourselves in the city? Are not our goods wasted? Have we enough wherewith to feed the people? Nay we will watch to-night and to-morrow we will fight. And if Achilles comes to the battle, I will meet him, for the gods give victory now to one man and now to another."

And the people clapped their hands, for they were foolish, and knew not what the morrow would bring forth.

---

[1] Editor's Note: Bier, a frame in which to carry a corpse. Of Germanic origin, to Old English: bēr. Not archaic, but used rarely after the 19th century.

CHAPTER XXI

THE MAKING OF THE ARMS

Meanwhile there was a great mourning for Patroclus in the camp of the Greeks. And Achilles stood up in the midst of the people and said: "Truly the gods do not fulfil the thoughts of men. Did I not say to the father of Patroclus that I would return with him, bringing back our portion of the spoils of Troy? And now he is dead; nor shall I return to the house of Peleus my father, for I too must die in this land. But I care not, if only I may have vengeance upon Hector. Truly I will not bury Patroclus till I can bring the head and the arms of Hector with which to honour him." So they washed the body of Patroclus, and put ointment into the wounds, and laid it on a bed, and covered with a linen cloth from the head to the feet, putting over the linen cloth a white robe. And all night the Myrmidons made lamentation for him.

Thetis went to the house of Hephaestus, who was the god of all them who worked in gold and silver and iron. She found him busy at his work, for he was making cauldrons for the palace of the gods. They had golden wheels underneath them with which they could run of themselves into the chambers of the palace, and come back of themselves as might be wanted. The Lady Grace who was wife to Hephaestus saw Thetis, and caught her by the hand, and said: "O Goddess, whom we love and honour, what business brings you here? Gladly will we serve you." And she led her into the house, and set her on a chair that was adorned with silver studs, and put a stool under her feet. Then she called to her husband, saying: "Thetis is here, and wants something from you. Come quickly." He answered: "Truly there could be no guest more welcome than Thetis. When my mother cast me out from her house because I was lame, then Thetis and her sister received me in their house under the sea. Nine years I dwelt with them, yes, and hammered many a trinket for them in a hollow cave that was close by. Truly I would give the price of my life to serve Thetis." Then he put away his tools, and washed himself, and took a staff in his hands and came into the house, and sat down upon a chair, and said: "Tell me all that is in your mind, for I will do all that you desire if only it can be done." Then Thetis told him of how her son Achilles had been put to shame by King Agamemnon, and of his anger, and of all that came to pass afterwards, and of how Patroclus had been slain in battle, and how the arms were lost. And having told this story, she said:

"Make for my son Achilles, I pray you, a shield, and a helmet, and greaves for his legs, and a breastplate."

"That will I do," answered Hephaestus, "I will make for him such arms as men will wonder at when they see them. Would that I could keep from him as easily the doom of death!"

So he went to his forge and turned the bellows to the fire, and bade them work, for they did not need a hand to work them. And he put copper and tin and gold and silver into the fire to make them soft, and set the anvil, and took the hammer in one hand and the tongs in the other.

First he made a shield, great and strong, with a silver belt by which a man might hold it. On it he made an image of the earth and the sky and the sea, with the sun, and the moon, and all the stars. Also he made images of two cities in one city there was peace, and in the other city there was war. In the city of peace they led a bride to the house of her husband with music and dancing, and the women stood in the door to see the show. And in another part of the same city the judges sat, to judge the case of a man who had been slain. One man said that he had paid the price of blood, for if one man slays another he must pay a price for him, and the other man said the price was not paid. Round about the city of war there was an army of besiegers and on the wall stood men defending it. Also the men of this same city had set an ambush by a river, at a place where the cattle came down to drink. And when the cattle came down the men that lay in ambush rose up quickly, and took them, and slew the herdsmen. And the army of the besiegers heard the cry, and rode on horses, and came quickly to the river and fought with the men who had taken the cattle. Also he made the image of one field in which men were ploughing, and of another in which reapers reaped the corn, and behind the reapers came boys who gathered the corn in their arms and bound it in sheaves, and at the top of the field stood the master, glad at heart because the harvest was good. Also he made a vineyard, and through the vineyard there was a path, and along the path went young men and maids bearing baskets of grapes, and in the midst stood a boy holding a harp of gold, who sang a pleasant song. Also he made a herd of oxen going from the stalls to the pasture; and close by two lions had laid hold of a great bull and were devouring it, and the dogs stood far off and barked. A sheep-fold also he made, and a dance of men and maids; the men wore daggers of gold hanging from silver belts, and the maids had gold crowns round their heads. And round about the shield he made ocean like to a great river. Also he made a breastplate, and a great helmet with a ridge of gold, in which the plumes should be set, and greaves of tin for the legs. When he had finished all his work, he gave the shield and the other things to Thetis. And she flew, swift as a hawk, to where her son abode by the ships. She found him lying on the ground, holding in his arms the body of Patroclus, weeping aloud, while his men lamented.

The goddess stood in the midst, and caught her son by the hand and said: "Come now, let us leave the dead man. It was the will of the gods that he should die. But you must think about other things. Come now and take this gift from Hephaestus, armour beautiful exceedingly, such as man has never yet worn."

And as she spoke, she cast the armour down at the feet of Achilles. It rattled loud as it fell, and it shone so brightly that the eyes of the Myrmidons were dazzled by it. But Achilles took up the arms from the ground, glad at heart to see them, and said: "Mother, these indeed are such arms as can be made in heaven only. Gladly will I put them on for the battle. Yet one thing troubles me. I fear lest decay should come on the body of Patroclus, before I can do it such honour as I desire."

But Thetis answered: "Let this not trouble you. I will keep the body from decay. But do you make peace with the king and prepare yourself for the battle." And she put precious things such as are known only in heaven into the nostrils of the dead man to keep him from decay.

CHAPTER XXII

THE QUARREL ENDED

A chilles went along by the ships, shouting with a loud voice to the Greeks that they should come to the battle. And they all came; there was not a man left, even those who had been used to stay behind, the men who looked after the ships, and they who had the care of the food. They all followed when Achilles came back to the war. And the chiefs came to the assembly, some of them, as Diomed and Ulysses and King Agamemnon himself, leaning on their spears because their wounds were fresh.

Achilles stood up and spoke: "It was a foolish thing, King Agamemnon, that we quarrelled about a girl. Many a Greek who is now dead had still been alive but for this, and the Trojans would not have profited by our loss. But let bygones be bygones. Here I make an end of my anger. Make haste, then, and call the Greeks to battle, and we will see whether the Trojans will fight by the ships or by their own walls."

Then King Agamemnon answered from the place where he sat: "Listen, ye Greeks. You have blamed me for this quarrel; yet it was not I, but the Fury who turns the thoughts of men to madness, that brought it about. Nevertheless it is for me to make amends. And this I will do, giving thee all the gifts which Ulysses promised in my name. Stay here till my people bring them from the ships." Achilles said: "Give the gifts, O King, if you are pleased so to do, or keep them for yourself. There is one thing only that I care for, to get to the battle without delay."

Then said the wise Ulysses: "Achilles, do not make the Greeks fight before they have eaten, for the battle will be long, because the gods have put courage into the hearts of the Trojans. A man who has not eaten cannot fight from morning to sunset, for his limbs grow weary, and he thinks about food and drink. Let us bid the people therefore disperse, and make ready a meal, and let King Agamemnon first send the gifts to your tent, and then let him make a feast, as is right when friends who have quarrelled make peace again." King Agamemnon answered: "You speak well, Ulysses. Do you yourself fetch the gifts, and my people shall make ready a feast." Achilles said: "How can I think of feasting when Patroclus lies dead? Let there be no delay, and let the Greeks sup well when they have driven the Trojans into their city. As for me, neither food nor drink shall pass my lips."

But Ulysses answered: "You are by far stronger than I am, O son of Peleus, but I am the older, and have seen many things. Ask not the Greeks to fast because of the dead. For men die every day, and every day would be a day of fasting. Rather let us bury our dead out of our sight, and mourn for them for a day, and then harden our hearts to forget. And let them who are left strengthen themselves with meat and drink, that they may fight the better."

Then Ulysses went to the ships of King Agamemnon and fetched thence the gifts, the cauldrons and the horses and the gold, and the women slaves, and chief of all the girl Briseis, and he took them to the tent of Achilles. And when Briseis saw Patroclus lying dead upon the couch, she beat her breast and her face and wailed aloud, for he had been gentle and good. And the other women wept with her, thinking each of her own troubles.

When the King and the chiefs would have had Achilles feast with them he refused. "I will not eat or drink," said he, "till I shall have had vengeance. Often, O Patroclus, have you made ready the meal when we were going to battle, and now you lie dead. I had not grieved so much if my old father or my only son had died. Often have I said to myself: 'I, indeed, shall die in this place, but Patroclus will go back and show my son all that was mine, goods and servants and palace.'"

And as he wept the old men wept with him, thinking each of those whom he had left at home.

Then the Greeks took their meal, the chiefs with King Agamemnon, and the others each with his own company. But Achilles sat fasting. Then Zeus said to Athene: "Do you not care for your dear Achilles? See how the other Greeks eat and drink, but he sits fasting." So Athene flew down from heaven, and poured heavenly food into the breast of Achilles that his strength might not fail for hunger. But he did not know what she did only he felt the new strength in him. Then he armed himself with the arms which Thetis brought to him from Hephaestus, and he took from its case the great Pelian spear which no man but he could wield. After this he climbed into his chariot, and he said to his horses: "Take care now, Bayard and Piebald, that you do not leave your master to-day, as you left Patroclus yesterday, dead on the field." Then Hera gave a voice to the horse Bayard, and he said: "It was not our fault, O Achilles, that Patroclus died. It was Apollo who slew him, but Hector had the glory. You too, some day, shall be slain by a god and a man." Achilles answered: "I know my doom, but I care not so that I may have vengeance on the Trojans."

CHAPTER XXIII

THE BATTLE AT THE RIVER

When the two armies were set in order against each other, Apollo said to Aeneas: "Aeneas, where are now your boastings that you would stand up against Achilles and fight with him?"

Aeneas answered: "That, indeed, I said long ago in days that are past. Once I stood up against him it was when he took the town of Lyrnessus. But he overcame me, and I fled before him, and but for my nimble feet I had been slain that day. Surely a god is with him, and makes his spear to fly so strongly and so straight."

But Apollo answered: "But if he is the son of a goddess, so also are you and, indeed, your mother is greater than his, for she is the child of Zeus, and Thetis is but a daughter of the Sea. Drive straight at him with your spear, and do not fear his fierce words and looks."

So Aeneas came forth out of the press to meet Achilles. And Achilles said to him: "What mean you, Aeneas? Do you think to slay me? Have the Trojans promised that they will have you for their king, or that they will give a choice portion of land, ploughland and orchard, if only you can prevail over me? You will not find it an easy thing. Have you forgotten the day when you fled before me at Lyrnessus?"

Aeneas said: "Son of Peleus, you will not frighten me with words, for I also am the son of a goddess. Come, let us try who is the better of us two."

So he cast his spear, and it struck full on the shield of Achilles, and made so dreadful a sound that the hero himself was frightened. But the shield that a god had made was not to be broken by the spear of a mortal man. It pierced, indeed, the first fold and the second, which were of bronze, but it was stopped by the third, which was of gold, and there were two more folds, and these of tin. Now Achilles threw his spear. Easily it pierced the shield of the Trojan, and though it did not wound him it came so near that he was deadly frightened. Yet he did not fly, for when Achilles drew his sword and rushed at him, he took up a great stone from the ground to throw at him. Nevertheless he would have been most certainly slain but for the help of the gods. For it was decreed that he and his children after him should reign in the time to come over the men of Troy. Therefore Poseidon himself, though for the most part he had no love for the Trojans, caught him up and carried him out of the battle; but first he took Achilles' spear out of the shield and laid it at the hero's feet. Much did he marvel to see it. "Here is a great wonder," he cried, "that I see with my eyes. My spear that I threw I see lying at my feet, but the man at whom I threw it I see not. Truly this Aeneas is dear to the gods."

Then he rushed into the battle, slaying as he went. Hector would have met him, but Apollo said: "Fight not with Achilles, for he is stronger than you and will slay you." So Hector stood aside. Yet when he saw the youngest of his brothers slain before his eyes, he could bear it no longer, and rushed to meet Achilles. Right glad was Achilles to see him, saying to himself: "The time is come; this is the man who killed Patroclus." And to Hector he said: "Come on and taste of death." But Hector answered: "You will not frighten me with words, son of Peleus, for though one man be stronger than another, yet it is Zeus who gives the victory."

Then he cast his spear, but Athene turned it aside with a breath. And when Achilles leapt upon him with a shout, then Apollo snatched him away. Three times did he leap at him, and three times he struck only the mist. The fourth time he cried with a terrible voice: "Dog, these four times you have escaped from death, but I shall meet you again when Apollo is not at hand to help you."

And now as the Trojans fled before Achilles, they came to the river they leapt into it till it was full of horses and men. Achilles left his spear upon the bank and rushed into the water, having only his sword. And the Trojans were like to fishes in the sea when they fly from a dolphin—in rocks and shallows they hide themselves, but the great beast devours them apace. There was but one man of them all who dared to stand up against him. When Achilles saw him he said, "And who are you that dare to stand up against me?" And the man said, "I am the son of Axius, the river god, and I come from the land of Paeonia." And as he spoke he cast two spears, one with each hand, for he could use both hands alike. The one struck on the shield and pierced two folds, but was stayed in the third, as the spear of Aeneas had been; with the other he grazed the right hand of Achilles, so that the blood gushed forth. Then Achilles cast his spear but missed his aim, and the spear stood fast in the river bank. Then the other laid hold of it and tried to drag it forth. Three times he tried, but could not move it; the fourth time he tried to break it. But as he tried Achilles slew him. Yet he had this glory that he alone wounded the great Achilles.

But Achilles had to fight not only with mortal men, but with the god of the river also. For when the god of the river saw that Achilles was slaying many both of the Trojans and of the allies, he took upon himself the form of a man, and said to Achilles: "Without doubt, O Achilles, you are the greatest warrior among all the sons of men; for not only are you stronger than all others, but the gods themselves help you and protect you. It may be that they have given you to destroy all the sons of Troy; nevertheless I require of you that you depart from me, and do that which you have to do upon the plain, for my streams are choked with the multitude of those whom you have slain, and I cannot pass to the sea."

Achilles answered: "I would not do anything that displeases you. Nevertheless I will make no end of slaying the Trojans till they have made their way into the city, or till I have come face to face with Hector, and either slay him or be slain, as the gods may please."

THE GODS DESCENDING TO BATTLE

Then Achilles turned again to the Trojans and slew still more of them. Then the River rose up against Achilles with all his might, and beat upon his shield, so that he could not stand upon his feet. He caught hold, therefore, of a lime tree that grew upon the bank; but the tree broke away from its place with all its roots, and lay across the river and stopped it from flowing, for it had many branches. Then Achilles was afraid, and climbed out of the water, and ran across the plain; but the River still followed him, for it wished to hinder him from destroying the men of Troy. For the Trojans were dear to the River because they honoured him with sacrifices. And though he was very swift of foot, it overtook him, for, indeed, the gods are mightier than men, and when he tried to stand up against it, it rushed upon him with a great wave up to his shoulders, and bowed his knees under him. Then Achilles lifted up his hands to heaven and cried: "Will no one of the gods have pity upon me and help me? Surely it would be better that Hector should slay me, for he is the bravest of men. This were better than that I should perish miserably as a boy whom a storm sweeps away when he is herding his cattle on the plain."

But the River raged yet more and more; and he called to another river his brother, for there were two that flowed across the plains of Troy, saying: "Brother, let us two stay the fury of this man, or he will surely destroy the city of Priam, which is dear to us. Fill your stream to the highest, and bring against him a great wave, with trunks of trees and bodies of men whom he has slain. So we will sweep him away, and his people will have no need to heap up a mound of earth over his bones, for we will cover him with sand."

But when Hera saw this, she cried to the Fire-god, her son: "Come near and help us, and bring much fire with you, and burn the trees upon the bank of the river, yea, and the river itself."

So the Fire-god lit a great fire. First it burnt all the dead bodies on the plain; next it burnt all the trees that were on the banks of the river, the limes and the willows and the tamarisks; also it burnt the water-plants that were in the river; the very fishes and eels it scorched, so that they twisted hither and thither in their pain. Then the River cried to the Fire-god: "Cease now from burning me; Achilles may do what he will with the Trojans. What do I care for mortal men?" So the Fire-god ceased from burning him, and the river troubled Achilles no more.

CHAPTER XXIV

THE SLAYING OF HECTOR

King Priam stood on a tower of the wall and saw how Achilles was driving the men of Troy before him, and his heart was much troubled within him, thinking how he could help his people. So he went down and spoke to those who kept the gates: "Keep now the wicket-gates open, holding them in your hand, that the people may enter by them, for they are flying before Achilles." So the keepers held the wicket-gates in their hands, and the people made haste to come in; they were wearied with toil and consumed with thirst, and Achilles followed close after them. And the Greeks would have taken the city of Troy that hour but that Apollo saved it, for the gates being open they could enter with the Trojans, whereas the gates being shut, the people were left to perish. And the way in which he saved the city was this. He put courage into the heart of Agenor, son to Antenor, standing also by him that he should not be slain. Agenor, therefore, stood thinking to himself: "Shall I flee with these others? Not so: for Achilles will overtake me, so swift of foot is he, and shall slay me, and I shall die the death of a coward. Or shall I flee across the plain to Mount Ida, and hide myself in the thicket, and come back to the city when it is dark? But if he see me, he will pursue me and overtake me. Shall I not rather stand here and meet him before the gates? For he too is a mortal man, and may be slain by the spear."

Therefore he stood by the gates waiting for Achilles, for Apollo had given him courage. And when Achilles came near Agenor cast his spear, and struck his leg beneath the knee, but the greave turned the spear, so strong was it, having been made by a god. But when Achilles rushed at him to slay him, Apollo lifted him up from the ground and set him safe within the walls. And that the men of Troy might have time to enter, the god took Agenor's shape and fled before Achilles, and Achilles pursued him. Meanwhile the Trojans flocked into the city through the wicket-gates, nor did they stay to ask who was safe and who was dead, so great was their fear and such their haste. Only Hector remained outside the city, in front of the great gates which were called the Scaean Gates. All the while Achilles was fiercely pursuing the false Agenor, till at last Apollo turned and spoke to him: "Why do you pursue me, swiftfooted Achilles? Have you not yet found out that I am a god, and that all your fury is in vain? And now all the Trojans are safe in the city, and you are here, far out of the way, seeking to kill one who cannot die."

Achilles answered him in great anger: "You have done me a great wrong in this. Surely of all the gods you are the one who loves mischief most. If it had not been for this many Trojans more would have fallen; but you have saved your favourites and robbed me of great glory. Oh that I could take vengeance on you! truly you would have paid dearly for your cheat."

Then he turned and ran towards the city, swift as a race-horse when it whirls a chariot across the plains. And his armour shone upon him as bright as Orion, which men call also the Dog, shines in the autumn, when the vintage is gathered, an evil light, bringing fevers to men. Old Priam saw him and groaned aloud, and stretched out his hands crying to Hector his son, where he stood before the gates waiting to fight with this terrible warrior:

"O my son, wait not for this man, lest he kill you, for indeed he is stronger than you. I would that the gods had such love for him as I have. Soon would he be food for dogs and vultures. Of many sons has he bereaved me, but if he should bereave me of you, then would not I only and the mother who bore you mourn, but every man and woman in Troy. Come within the walls, my dear son, come, for you are the hope of the city. Come, lest an evil fate come upon me in my old age, that I should see my sons slain with the sword and my daughters carried into captivity, and the babes dashed upon the ground."

So spoke old Priam, but he could not move the heart of his son. Then from the other side of the wall his mother, Queen Hecuba, cried to him. She wept aloud, and hoping that she might so persuade him, said: "O Hector, my son, have pity on me. Think of the breast which in old days I gave you, when you were hungry, and stilled your crying. Come, I beseech you, inside the walls, and do not wait for him, or stand up in battle against him. For if he conquers you, then not only will you die, but dogs and vultures will eat your flesh far from here, by the ships of the Greeks."

But all her prayers were in vain, for he was still minded to await the coming of Achilles, and stand up to him in battle. And as he waited many thoughts passed through his mind: "Woe is me, if I go within the walls! Will not they reproach me who gave me good advice which I would not hear, saying that I should bring the people within the walls, when the great Achilles roused himself to the battle? Would that I had done this thing! it had been by far better for us; but now I have destroyed the people. I fear the sons and daughters of Troy, lest they should say: 'Hector trusted in his strength, and he has brought the people whom he should have saved to harm.' It would be far better for me to stay here and meet the great Achilles, and either slay him, or, if it must be so, be slain by him. Or shall I lay down my shield and take off my helmet and lean my spear against the wall, and go to meet him and say: 'We will give back the Fair Helen and all the riches which Paris carried off with her; also we will give all the precious things that there are in the city that the Greeks may divide them among themselves, taking an oath that we are keeping nothing back, if only you will leave us in peace'? But this is idle talk. He will have neither shame nor pity, and will slay me as I stand without defence before him. No: it is better far to meet in arms and see whether Zeus will give the victory to him or to me."

These were the things which Hector thought in his heart. And Achilles came near, shaking over his right shoulder the great Pelian spear, and the flashing of his arms was like to fire or to the sun when it rises. But Hector trembled when he saw him, and his heart failed him so that he turned his back and fled. Fast he fled from the place where he stood by the great Scaean Gate, and fast did Achilles pursue him, just as a hawk, which is more swift than all other birds, pursues a dove among the hills. The two ran past the watch-tower, and past the wild fig tree, along the wagon-road which ran round the walls, till they came to the springs from which the river rises. Two springs there were, one hot as though it had been heated with fire, and the other cold, cold as ice or snow, even in the summer. There were two basins of stone in which the daughters of Troy had been used to wash their garments; but that was in the old days, when there was peace, before the Greeks came to the land. Past the springs they ran; it was no race which men run for some prize, a sheep, maybe, or an ox-hide shield. Rather the prize was the life of Hector. So they ran round the city, and the Trojans on the wall and the Greeks upon the plain looked on. And the gods looked on as they sat in their palace on the top of Olympus. And Zeus said:

"Now this is a piteous thing which I see. My heart is grieved for Hector—Hector, who has never failed to honour me and the other gods with sacrifice. See how the great Achilles is pursuing him! Come, let us take counsel together. Shall we save him from death, or shall we let him fall by the spear of Achilles?" Athene said: "What is this that you purpose? Will you save a man whom the fates appoint to die? Do this, if you will, but the other gods do not approve."

Then said Zeus: "This is a thing that I hate; but be it as you will." All this time Hector still fled, and Achilles still pursued. Hector sought for shelter in the walls, and Achilles ever drove him towards the plain. Just as in a dream, when one seems to fly and another seems to pursue, and the first cannot escape, neither can the second overtake, so these two ran. Yet Apollo helped Hector, giving strength to his knees, else he had not held out against Achilles, than whom there was no faster runner among the sons of men. Three times did they run round the city, but when they came for the fourth time to the springs Athene lighted from the air close to Achilles and said: "This is your day of glory, for you shall slay Hector, though he be a mighty warrior. It is his doom to die, and Apollo's self shall not save him. Stand here and take breath, and I will make him meet you."

So Achilles stood leaning on his spear. And Athene took the shape of Deïphobus, and came near to Hector and said to him: "My brother, Achilles presses you hard; but come, we two will stand up against him." Hector answered, "O Deïphobus, I have always loved you above all my brothers, and now I love you still more, for you only have come to my help, while they remain within the walls." Then said Deïphobus: "Much did my father and my mother and my comrades entreat me to stay within the walls, but I would not, for I could not bear to leave you alone. Come, therefore, let us fight this man together, and see whether he will carry our spoils to the ships or we shall slay him here."

Then Hector said to Achilles: "Three times have you pursued me round the walls, and I dared not stand against you, but now I fear you no more. Only let us make this covenant. If Zeus gives me the victory to-day, I will give back your body to the Greeks, only I will keep your arms: do you, therefore, promise to do the same with me?"

Achilles frowned at him and said: "Hector, talk not of covenants to me. Men and lions make no oaths to each other, neither is there any agreement between wolves and sheep. Make no delay; let us fight together, that I may have vengeance for the blood of all my comrades whom thou hast slain, and especially of Patroclus, the man whom I loved beyond all others."

Then he threw the great spear, but Hector saw it coming and avoided it, crouching down so that the spear flew over his head and fixed itself in the ground. But Athene snatched it up and gave it back to Achilles; but this Hector did not see. Then said Hector to Achilles: "You have missed your aim, Achilles. Now see whether I have not a truer aim."

Then he cast his spear, and the aim, indeed, was true, for it struck full upon the shield; it struck, but it bounded far away. Then he cried to Deïphobus: "Give me another spear;" but lo! Deïphobus was gone. Then he knew that his end was come, and he said to himself: "The gods have brought my doom upon me. I thought that Deïphobus was with me; but he is behind the walls, and this was but a cheat with which Athene cheated me. Nevertheless, if I must die, let me at least die in the doing of such a deed as men shall remember in the years to come."

So he spoke, and drew his great sword, and rushed upon Achilles as an eagle rushes down from the clouds upon its prey. But never a blow did he deal for Achilles ran to meet him, holding his shield before him, and the plumes of his helmet streamed behind him as he ran, and the point of his spear was as bright as the evening star. For a moment he doubted where he should drive it home, for the armour of Patroclus which Hector wore guarded him well. But a spot there was, where the stroke of spear or sword is deadliest, by the collar-bone where the neck joins the shoulder. There he drove in the spear, and the point stood out behind the neck, and Hector fell in the dust. Then Achilles cried aloud: "Hector, you thought not of me when you slew Patroclus and spoiled him of his arms. But now you have fallen, and the dogs and vultures shall eat your flesh, but to him the Greeks will give honourable burial."

But Hector said, his voice now growing faint: "O Achilles, I entreat you, by all that you hold dear, to give my body to my father and mother that they may duly bury it. Large ransoms will they pay of gold and silver and bronze."

"Speak not to me of ransom," said Achilles. "Priam shall not buy thee back, no, not for your weight in gold."

Then Hector said: "I know you well, what manner of man you are, and that the heart in your breast is of iron. Only beware lest the anger of the gods come upon you for such deeds in the days when Paris and Apollo shall slay you hard by these very gates."

So speaking, he died. And Achilles said: "Die, dog that you are; but my doom I will meet when it shall please the gods to send it."

ANDROMACHE FAINTING ON THE WALL

Then did Achilles devise a cruel thing. He pierced the ankle-bones of the dead man, and fastened the body with thongs of ox-hide to the chariot, and so dragged it to the ships.

Now Andromache knew nothing of what had come to pass. She sat in her house weaving a great mantle, embroidered with flowers. And she bade her maidens make ready the bath for Hector, when he should come back from the battle, knowing not that he would never need it anymore. Then there rose a great cry of wailing from the walls, and she rose up from her weaving in great haste, and dropped the shuttle from her hands and said to the maids: "Come now, I must see what has happened, for I fear that some evil has come to the men of Troy. Maybe Hector is in danger, for he is always bold, and will fight in the front."

Then she ran along the street to the walls like to a madwoman. And when she came to the walls she looked, and lo! the horses of Achilles were dragging the body of Hector to the ships. Then a sudden darkness came upon her, and she fell to the ground as though she were dead.

CHAPTER XXV

THE RANSOMING OF HECTOR

The Greeks made a great mourning for Patroclus, and paid due honours to him, but the body of Hector was shamefully treated, for Achilles caused it to be dragged daily about the tomb of his friend. Then Zeus sent for Thetis and said to her: "Go to the camp, and bid your son give up the body of Hector for ransom; it angers me to see him do dishonour to the dead."

So Thetis went to the tent of Achilles and found him weeping softly for his friend, for the strength of his sorrow was now spent. And she said to him: "It is the will of Zeus that you give up the body of Hector for ransom." And he said: "Let it be so, if the gods will have it."

Then, again, Zeus sent Iris his messenger to King Priam, where he sat in his palace with his face wrapped in his mantle, and his sons weeping round him, and his daughter and his daughters-in-law wailing in their chambers of the palace. Iris said to him: "Be of good cheer; I come from Zeus. He bids you take precious gifts wherewith to buy back the body of Hector from Achilles. Nor will Achilles refuse to give it."

So Priam rose up from his place with gladness in his heart. Nor would he listen to the Queen when she would have kept him back.

"I have heard the voice of the messenger of Zeus, and I will go. And if I die, what do I care? Let Achilles slay me, so that I hold the body of my son once more in my arms."

Then he caused precious things to be put into a wagon, mantles which had never been washed, and rugs, and cloaks, twelve of each, and ten talents of gold, and cauldrons and basins, and a great cup of gold which the Thracians had given him. Nothing of his treasures did he spare if only he might buy back his son. Then he bade his sons yoke the mules to the wagon. With many bitter words did he speak to them; they were cowards, he said, an evil brood, speakers of lying words, and mighty only to drink wine. But they did not answer him. Then Priam himself yoked the horses to the chariot, the herald helping. But before he went he poured out wine to Zeus, and prayed, saying: "Hear me, O Father, and cause Achilles to pity me; give me also a lucky sign that I may go on this business with a good heart."

So Zeus sent an eagle, a mighty bird, and it flew with wings outstretched over the city, on the right hand of the King.

Then the King passed out of the gates. Before him the mules drew the wagon, these the herald drove. But Priam

**HECTOR'S BODY DRAGGED BY
THE CHARIOT OF ACHILLES**

himself drove his horses. Then said Zeus to Hermes: "Go, guide the King, so that none of the Greeks may see him before he comes to the tent of Achilles." So Hermes fastened on his feet the winged sandals with which he flies, and flew till he came to the plain of Troy. And when the wagon and the chariot were close to the tomb of Ilus, the herald spied a man (for Hermes had taken the shape of a man), and said to the King: "What shall we do? I see a man. Shall we flee, or shall we beg him to have mercy on us?" And the King was greatly troubled. But Hermes came near and said: "Whither do you go in the darkness with these horses and mules? Have you no fear of the Greeks? If anyone should spy all this wealth, what then? You are old, and could scarcely defend yourselves. But be of good cheer; I will protect you, for you are like to my own dear father."

Priam answered: "Happy is he to have such a son. Surely the gods are with me, that I have met such a one as you."

Then said Hermes: "Tell me true; are you sending away these treasures for safe keeping, fearing that the city will be taken now that Hector is dead?"

Priam answered: "Who are you that you speak of Hector?"

Hermes said: "I am a Myrmidon, one of the people of Achilles, and often have I seen your son in the front of the battle."

Then the King asked him: "Is the body of Hector yet whole, or have the dogs and vultures devoured it?"

Hermes answered: "It is whole and without blemish, as fresh as when he died. Surely the gods love him, even though he be dead."

Then King Priam would have had the young man take a gift; but Hermes said: "I will take no gift unknown to my master. So to do would be to wrong him. But I will guide you to his tent, if you would go thither."

So he leapt into the chariot and took the reins. And when they came to the trench, where the sentinels were at their meal, Hermes caused a deep sleep to fall on them, and he opened the gate, and brought in the King with his treasures. And when they were at the tent of Achilles, the young man said: "I am Hermes, whom Father Zeus sent to be your guide. Go in and clasp him about the knees, and entreat him to have pity upon you." And he vanished out of his sight.

Then Priam went into the tent, where Achilles, who had just ended his meal, sat at the table, and caught his knees and kissed his hands, yea, the very hands which had slain so many of his sons. He said: "Have pity on me, O Achilles, thinking of your own father. He is old as I am, yet it goes well with him, so long as he knows that you are alive, for he hopes to see you coming back from the land of Troy. But as for me, I am altogether miserable. Many sons have I lost, and now the best of them all is dead, and lo! I kiss the hands which slew him."

Then the heart of Achilles was moved with pity and he wept, thinking now of his old father and now of the dead Patroclus. At last he stood up from his seat and said: "How did you dare to come to my tent, old man? Surely you must have a heart of iron. But come, sit and eat and drink; for this a man must do, for all the sorrows that come upon him."

But the King said: "Ask me not to eat and drink while my

son lies unburied and without honour. Rather take the gifts which I have brought, with which to ransom him."

But Achilles frowned and said: "Vex me not: I am minded to give back the body of Hector, but let me go my own way." Then Priam held his peace, for he feared to rouse the anger of Achilles. Then Achilles went forth from the tent, and two companions with him. First they took the gifts from the wagon only they left two cloaks and a tunic wherewith to cover the dead. And Achilles bade the women wash and anoint the body, only that they should do this apart from the tent, lest Priam should see his son, and lament aloud and so wake the fury in his heart. And when the body was washed and anointed, Achilles himself lifted it in his arms, and put it on a litter, and his comrades put the litter in the wagon.

When all was finished, Achilles groaned and cried to his dead friend, saying: "Be not angry, O Patroclus, that I have given the body of Hector to his father. He has given a noble ransom, and of this you shall have your share as is meet."

Then he went back to his tent and said: "Your son, old man, is ransomed, and to-morrow shall you see him and take him back to Troy. But now let us eat and drink." And this they did. But when this had ended, they sat and looked at each other, and Achilles wondered at King Priam, so noble was he to behold, and Priam wondered to see how strong and how fair was Achilles.

Then Priam said: "Let me sleep, Achilles, for I have not slept since my son was slain." So they made up for him a bed, but not in the tent, lest, perhaps, one of the chiefs should come in and see him. But before he slept the King said: "Let there be a truce for nine days between the Greeks and the Trojans, that we may bury Hector." And Achilles said: "It shall be so; I will stay the war for so long."

But when the King slept, Hermes came again to him and said: "Do you sleep among your enemies, O Priam? Awake and depart, for though Achilles has taken ransom for Hector, what would not your sons have to pay for you if the Greeks should find you in the camp?"

Then the old man rose up. And the wise herald yoked the mules to the wagon and the horses to the chariot. And they passed through the camp of the Greeks, no man knowing, and came safe to the city of Troy.

On the ninth day the King and his people made a great burying for Hector, such as had never before been seen in the land of Troy.

CHAPTER XXVI

THE END OF TROY

After these things came Memnon, a black warrior, who men said was the son of the Morning. He slew Antilochus, son of Nestor, and was himself slain by Achilles. Not many days afterwards Achilles himself was slain near the Scaen Gates. It was by an arrow from the bow of Paris that he was killed, but the arrow was guided by Apollo.

Yet Troy was not taken. Then Helenus, the seer, having been taken prisoner by Ulysses, said: "You cannot take the city till you bring the man who has the arrows of Hercules." So they fetched the man, and he killed many Trojans with the arrows, and among them Paris, who was the cause of all this trouble.

Last of all the Greeks devised this plan. Some of the bravest of the chiefs hid themselves in a great horse of wood, and the rest made a pretence of going away, but went no further than to an island hard by. And when the Trojans had dragged the horse into the city, thinking that it was an offering to the gods of the city, the chiefs let themselves out of it by night, and the other Greeks having come back, took the city in the tenth year from the beginning of the siege.

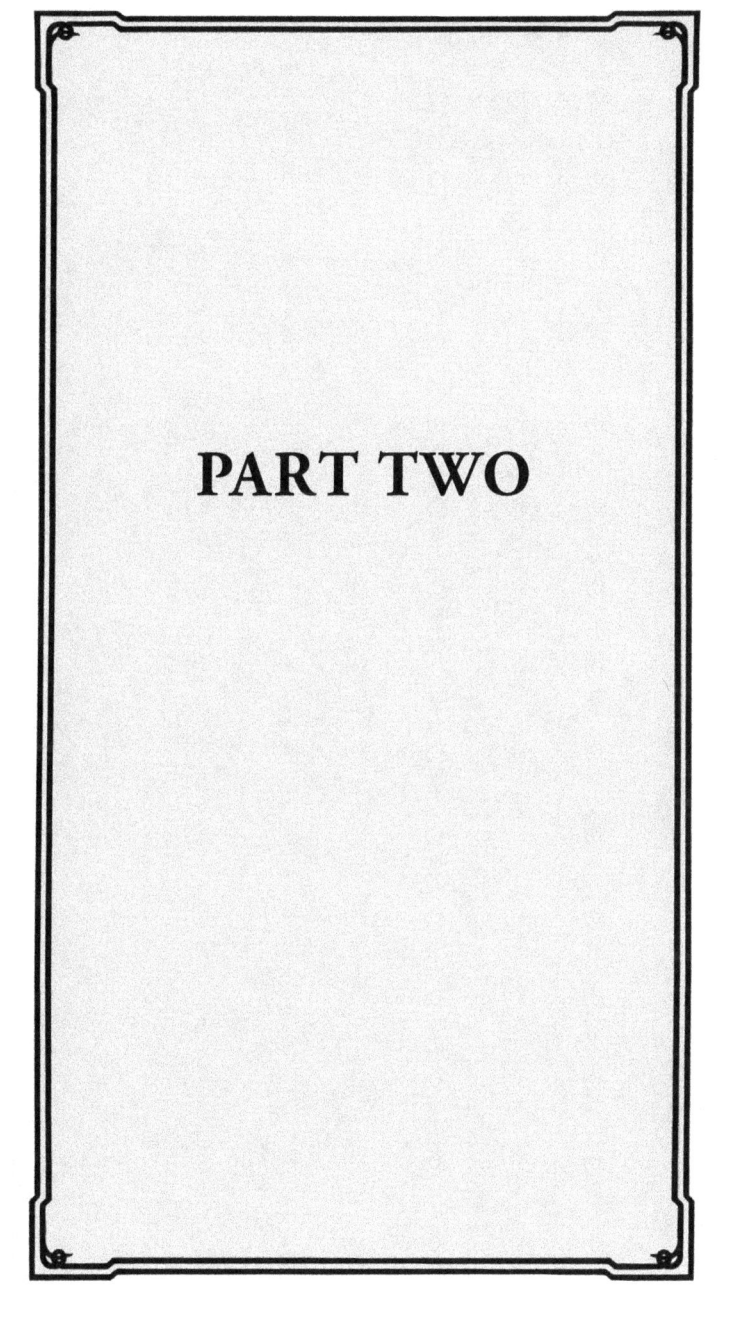

PART TWO

102

Ο Μ Η Ρ Ο Υ

ΒΑΤΡΑΧΟΜΥΟΜΑΧΙΑ.

Ἀρχόμῳ@, πρῶτον, Μυσῶν χορὸν ἐξ Ἑλικῶν@
Ἐλθεῖν εἰς ἐμὸν ἦτορ ἐπεύχομαι, εἵνεκ ἀοιδῆς,
Ἣν νέον ἐν δέλτοισιν ἐμοῖς ἐπὶ γούνασι θῆκα·
Δῆριν ἀπειρεσίῳ, πολεμίκλονον ἔργον Ἄρη@,
Εὐχόμῳ@ μερόπεσσιν ἐς ὄατα πᾶσι βαλέοθαι·
Πῶς μύες ἐν βατράχοισιν ἀριστεύσαντες ἔβησαν,
Γηγενέων ἀνδρῶν μιμεύμονοι ἔργα γιγάντων,
Ὡς λόγ@ ἐν θνητοῖσιν ἔλυ· πόλιν δ᾽ ἔχεν ἀρχίω.

Μῦς ποτὲ διψαλέ@, γαλέης κίνδυνον ἀλύξας,
Πλησίον ἐν λίμνη ἁπαλὸν προσέθηκε γλῶσιν,
Ὕδατι τερπόμῳ@ μελιηδέϊ· τὴν δὲ κατεῖδε
Λιμνόχαρις πολύφημ@, ἔπ@ δ᾽ ἐφθέγξατο τοῖν·
Ξεῖνε

First page of the *Batrachomyomachia*, 1726

Βατραχομυομαχία

Three Translations of
The Batrachomyomachia
THE BATTLE OF THE FROGS AND MICE

Rendered Unto English

By:

Hugh G. Evelyn-White, 1914

William Cowper, 1791

George Chapman, 1624

The attribution to Homer was disputed in antiquity and is to this day.

Opening Lines in Ancient Greek

Ἀρχόμενος πρώτης σελίδος χορὸν ἐξ Ἑλικῶνος

ἐλθεῖν εἰς ἐμὸν ἦτορ ἐπεύχομαι εἵνεκ ἀοιδῆς,

ἣν νέον ἐν δέλτοισιν ἐμοῖς ἐπὶ γούνασι θῆκα,

δῆριν ἀπειρεσίην, πολεμόκλονον ἔργον Ἄρηος,

εὐχόμενος μερόπεσσιν ἐς οὔατα πᾶσι βαλέσθαι

πῶς μύες ἐν βατράχοισιν ἀριστεύσαντες ἔβησαν,

γηγενέων ἀνδρῶν μιμούμενοι ἔργα Γιγάντων,

ὡς λόγος ἐν θνητοῖσιν ἔην· τοίην δ ἔχεν ἀρχήν.

Μῦς ποτε διψαλέος γαλέης κίνδυνον ἀλύξας,

Βατραχομυομαχία

πλησίον ἐν λίμνῃ λίχνον προσέθηκε γένειον...

———————◄◆►———————

THE BATTLE OF THE FROGS AND MICE

Translated by

Hugh G. Evelyn-White

1914

(ll. 1-8) Here I begin: and first I pray the choir of the Muses to come down from Helicon into my heart to aid the lay[1] which I have newly written in tablets upon my knee. Fain[2] would I sound in all men's ears that awful strife, that clamorous deed of war, and tell how the Mice proved their valour on the Frogs and rivalled the exploits of the Giants, those earth-born men, as the tale was told among mortals. Thus did the war begin.

---

[1] Editor's Note: Lay: a short poem that often tells a story of heroic adventures or romance; especially popular in medieval England and France.
[2] Editor's Note: Fain: (archaic) gladly.

(ll. 9-12) One day a thirsty Mouse who had escaped the ferret, dangerous foe, set his soft muzzle to the lake's brink and revelled in the sweet water. There a loud-voiced pond-larker spied him: and uttered such words as these.

(ll. 13-23) 'Stranger, who are you? Whence come you to this shore, and who is he who begot you? Tell me all this truly and let me not find you lying. For if I find you worthy to be my friend, I will take you to my house and give you many noble gifts such as men give to their guests. I am the king Puff-jaw, and am honoured in all the pond, being ruler of the Frogs continually. The father that brought me up was Mud-man who mated with Waterlady by the banks of Eridanus. I see, indeed, that you are well-looking and stouter than the ordinary, a king and a warrior in fight; but, come, make haste and tell me your descent.'

(ll. 24-55) Then Crumb-snatcher answered him and said: 'Why do you ask my race, which is well-known amongst all, both men and gods and the birds of heaven? Crumb-snatcher am I called, and I am the son of Bread-nibbler— he was my stout-hearted father—and my mother was Queen-licker, the daughter of Ham-gnawer the king: she bare me in the mouse-hole and nourished me with food, figs and nuts and dainties of all kinds. But how are you to make me your friend, who am altogether different in nature? For you get your living in the water, but I am used to eat such foods as men have: I never miss the thrice-kneaded loaf in its neat, round basket, or the thin-wrapped cake full of sesame and cheese, or the slice of ham, or liver vested in white fat, or cheese just curdled from sweet milk, or delicious honey-cake which even the blessed gods long for, or any of all those cakes which cooks make for the feasts of mortal men, larding their pots and pans with spices of all kinds. I gnaw no radishes and cabbages and pumpkins, nor feed on green leeks and parsley; for these are food for you who live in the lake. In battle I have never flinched from the cruel onset, but plunged straight into the fray and fought among the foremost. I fear not man though he has a big body, but run along his bed and bite the tip of his toe and nibble at his heel; and the man feels no hurt and his sweet sleep is not broken by my biting. But there are two things I fear above all else the whole world over, the hawk and the ferret—for these bring great grief on me—and the piteous trap wherein is treacherous death. Most of all I fear the ferret of the keener sort which follows you still even when you dive down your hole.'

(ll. 56-64) Then Puff-jaw answered him with a smile: 'Stranger you boast too much of belly-matters: we too have many marvels to be seen both in the lake and on the shore. For the Son of Chronos has given us Frogs the power to lead a double life, dwelling at will in two separate elements; and so we both leap on land and plunge beneath the water. If you would learn of all these things, 'tis easy done: just mount upon my back and hold me tight lest you be lost, and so you shall come rejoicing to my house.'

(ll. 65-81) So said he, and offered his back. And the Mouse mounted at once, putting his paws upon the other's sleek neck and vaulting nimbly. Now at first, while he still saw the land near by, he was pleased, and was delighted with Puff-jaw's swimming; but when dark waves began to wash over him, he wept loudly and blamed his unlucky change of mind: he tore his fur and tucked his paws in against his belly, while within him his heart quaked by reason of the strangeness: and he longed to get to land, groaning terribly through the stress of chilling fear. He put out his tail upon the water and worked it like a steering oar, and prayed to heaven that he might get to land. But when the dark waves washed over him he cried aloud and said: 'Not in such wise did the bull bear on his back the beloved load, when be brought Europa across the sea to Crete, as this Frog carries me over the water to his house, raising his yellow back in the pale water.'

(ll. 82-92) Then suddenly a water-snake appeared, a horrid sight for both alike, and held his neck upright above the water. And when he saw it, Puff-jaw dived at once, and never thought how helpless a friend he would leave perishing; but down to the bottom of the lake he went, and escaped black death. But the Mouse, so deserted, at once fell on his back, in the water. He wrung his paws and squeaked in agony of death: many times he sank beneath the water and many times he rose up again kicking. But he could not escape his doom, for his wet fur weighed him down heavily. Then at the last, as he was dying, he uttered these words.

(ll. 93-98) 'Ah, Puff-jaw, you shall not go unpunished for this treachery! You threw me, a castaway, off your body as from a rock. Vile coward! On land you would not have been the better man, boxing, or wrestling, or running; but now you have tricked me and cast me in the water. Heaven has an avenging eye, and surely the host of Mice will punish you and not let you escape.'

(ll. 99-109) With these words he breathed out his soul upon the water. But Lick-platter as he sat upon the soft bank saw him die and, raising a dreadful cry, ran and told the Mice.

And when they heard of his fate, all the Mice were seized with fierce anger, and bade their heralds summon the people to assemble towards dawn at the house of Bread-nibbler, the father of hapless Crumb-snatcher who lay outstretched on the water face up, a lifeless corpse, and no longer near the bank, poor wretch, but floating in the midst of the deep. And when the Mice came in haste at dawn, Bread-nibbler stood up first, enraged at his son's death, and thus he spoke.

(ll. 110-121) 'Friends, even if I alone had suffered great wrong from the Frogs, assuredly this is a first essay[1] at mischief for you all. And now I am pitiable, for I have lost three sons. First the abhorred ferret seized and killed one of them, catching him outside the hole; then ruthless men dragged another to his doom when by unheard-of arts they had contrived a wooden snare, a destroyer of Mice, which they call a trap. There was a third whom I and his dear mother loved well, and him Puff-jaw has carried out into the deep and drowned. Come, then, and let us arm ourselves and go out against them when we have arrayed ourselves in rich-wrought arms.'

(ll. 122-131) With such words he persuaded them all to gird themselves. And Ares who has charge of war equipped them. First they fastened on greaves and covered their shins with green bean-pods broken into two parts which they had gnawed out, standing over them all night. Their breast plates were of skin stretched on reeds, skilfully made from a

---

[1] Editor's Note: In this context, "his first essay" means "first trial or attempt." From the French word "essai."

ferret they had flayed. For shields each had the centre-piece of a lamp, and their spears were long needles all of bronze, the work of Ares, and the helmets upon their temples were pea-nut shells.

(ll. 132-138) So the Mice armed themselves. But when the Frogs were aware of it, they rose up out of the water and coming together to one place gathered a council of grievous war. And while they were asking whence the quarrel arose, and what the cause of this anger, a herald drew near bearing a wand in his paws, Pot-visitor the son of great-hearted Cheese-carver. He brought the grim message of war, speaking thus:

(ll. 139-143) 'Frogs, the Mice have sent me with their threats against you, and bid you arm yourselves for war and battle; for they have seen Crumb-snatcher in the water whom your king Puff-jaw slew. Fight, then, as many of you as are warriors among the Frogs.'

(ll. 144-146) With these words he explained the matter. So when this blameless speech came to their ears, the proud Frogs were disturbed in their hearts and began to blame Puff-jaw. But he rose up and said:

(ll. 147-159) 'Friends, I killed no Mouse, nor did I see one perishing. Surely he was drowned while playing by the lake and imitating the swimming of the Frogs, and now these wretches blame me who am guiltless. Come then; let us take counsel how we may utterly destroy the wily Mice. Moreover, I will tell you what I think to be the best. Let us all gird on our armour and take our stand on the very brink of the lake, where the ground breaks down sheer: then when they come out and charge upon us, let each seize by the crest the

Mouse who attacks him, and cast them with their helmets into the lake; for so we shall drown these dry-hobs[1] in the water, and merrily set up here a trophy of victory over the slaughtered Mice.'

(ll. 160-167) By this speech he persuaded them to arm themselves. They covered their shins with leaves of mallows, and had breastplates made of fine green beet-leaves, and cabbage-leaves, skilfully fashioned, for shields. Each one was equipped with a long, pointed rush for a spear, and smooth snail-shells to cover their heads. Then they stood in close-locked ranks upon the high bank, waving their spears, and were filled, each of them, with courage.

(ll. 168-173) Now Zeus called the gods to starry heaven and showed them the martial throng and the stout warriors so many and so great, all bearing long spears; for they were as the host of the Centaurs and the Giants. Then he asked with a sly smile; 'Who of the deathless gods will help the Frogs and who the Mice?'

And he said to Athena;

(ll. 174-176) 'My daughter, will you go aid the Mice? For they all frolic about your temple continually, delighting in the fat of sacrifice and in all kinds of food.'

(ll. 177-196) So then said the son of Cronos. But Athena answered him: 'I would never go to help the Mice when they are hard pressed, for they have done me much mischief, spoiling my garlands and my lamps too, to get the oil. And

---

[1] Editor's Note: Not a direct translation from the Greek work, but a scornful epithet. The original text uses the Greek word "ξηρακοιτοι" which means "lying in dry places."

this thing that they have done vexes my heart exceedingly: they have eaten holes in my sacred robe, which I wove painfully spinning a fine woof on a fine warp, and made it full of holes. And now the money-lender is at me and charges me interest which is a bitter thing for immortals. For I borrowed to do my weaving, and have nothing with which to repay. Yet even so I will not help the Frogs; for they also are not considerable: once, when I was returning early from war, I was very tired, and though I wanted to sleep, they would not let me even doze a little for their outcry; and so I lay sleepless with a headache until cock-crow. No, gods, let us refrain from helping these hosts, or one of us may get wounded with a sharp spear; for they fight hand to hand, even if a god comes against them. Let us rather all amuse ourselves watching the fight from heaven.'

(ll. 197-198) So said Athena. And the other gods agreed with her, and all went in a body to one place.

(ll. 199-201) Then gnats with great trumpets sounded the fell [1] note of war, and Zeus the son of Cronos thundered from heaven, a sign of grievous battle.

(ll. 202-223) First Loud-croaker wounded Lickman in the belly, right through the midriff. Down fell he on his face and soiled his soft fur in the dust: he fell with a thud and his armour clashed about him. Next Troglodyte [2] shot at the son

---

[1] Editor's Note Archaic use of "fell," meaning grim, cruel, deadly. Still used in the expression "one fell swoop."

[2] Editor's Note: Troglodyte: The ancient meaning is "cave dweller" and was used by Herodatus to describe an ancient Ethiopian people who lived in caves. Today it is a pejorative term used to describe someone ignorant or crude. Note also that the scientific name for the Chimpanzee is *Pan troglodytes*.

of Mudman, and drove the strong spear deep into his breast; so he fell, and black death seized him and his spirit flitted forth from his mouth. Then Beety struck Pot-visitor to the heart and killed him, and Bread-nibbler hit Loud-crier in the belly, so that he fell on his face and his spirit flitted forth from his limbs. Now when Pond-larker saw Loud-crier perishing, he struck in quickly and wounded Troglodyte in his soft neck with a rock like a mill-stone, so that darkness veiled his eyes. Thereat Ocimides was seized with grief, and struck out with his sharp reed and did not draw his spear back to him again, but felled his enemy there and then. And Lickman shot at him with a bright spear and hit him unerringly in the midriff. And as he marked Cabbage-eater running away, he fell on the steep bank, yet even so did not cease fighting but smote that other so that he fell and did not rise again; and the lake was dyed with red blood as he lay outstretched along the shore, pierced through the guts and shining flanks. Also he slew Cheese-eater on the very brink...

((LACUNA))[1]

(ll. 224-251) But Reedy took to flight when he saw Ham-nibbler, and fled, plunging into the lake and throwing away his shield. Then blameless Pot-visitor killed Brewer and Water-larked killed the lord Ham-nibbler, striking him on the head with a pebble, so that his brains flowed out at his nostrils and the earth was bespattered with blood. Faultless Muck-coucher sprang upon Lick-platter and killed him with

---

[1] Editor's Note: Lacuna: unfilled space or gap; a missing section in a manuscript. In general, scholars consider the *Batrachomyomachia* to be complete, but with some inconsistencies in the text. Oxford Latin Dictionary. www.oxfordre.com. 12/22/2015

his spear and brought darkness upon his eyes: and Leeky saw it, and dragged Lick-platter by the foot, though he was dead, and choked him in the lake. But Crumb-snatcher was fighting to avenge his dead comrades, and hit Leeky before he reached the land; and he fell forward at the blow and his soul went down to Hades. And seeing this, the Cabbage-climber took a clod of mud and hurled it at the Mouse, plastering all his forehead and nearly blinding him. Thereat Crumb-snatcher was enraged and caught up in his strong hand a huge stone that lay upon the ground, a heavy burden for the soil: with that he hit Cabbage-climber below the knee and splintered his whole right shin, hurling him on his back in the dust. But Croakperson kept him off, and rushing at the Mouse in turn, hit him in the middle of the belly and drove the whole reed-spear into him, and as he drew the spear back to him with his strong hand, all his foe's bowels gushed out upon the ground. And when Troglodyte saw the deed, as he was limping away from the fight on the river bank, he shrank back sorely moved, and leaped into a trench to escape sheer death. Then Bread-nibbler hit Puff-jaw on the toes—he came up at the last from the lake and was greatly distressed...

((LACUNA))

(ll. 252-259) And when Leeky saw him fallen forward, but still half alive, he pressed through those who fought in front and hurled a sharp reed at him; but the point of the spear was stayed and did not break his shield. Then noble Rueful, like Ares himself, struck his flawless head-piece made of four pots—he only among the Frogs showed prowess in the throng. But when he saw the other rush at him, he did not stay to meet the stout-hearted hero but dived down to the depths of the lake.

(ll. 260-271) Now there was one among the Mice, Slice-snatcher, who excelled the rest, dear son of Gnawer the son of blameless Bread-stealer. He went to his house and bade his son take part in the war. This warrior threatened to destroy the race of Frogs utterly (3), and splitting a chestnut-husk into two parts along the joint, put the two hollow pieces as armour on his paws: then straightway the Frogs were dismayed and all rushed down to the lake, and he would have made good his boast—for he had great strength—had not the Son of Cronos, the Father of men and gods, been quick to mark the thing and pitied the Frogs as they were perishing. He shook his head, and uttered this word:

(ll. 272-276) 'Dear, dear, how fearful a deed do my eyes behold! Slice-snatcher makes no small panic rushing to and fro among the Frogs by the lake. Let us then make all haste and send warlike Pallas or even Ares, for they will stop his fighting, strong though he is.'

(ll. 277-284) So said the Son of Cronos; but Hera answered him: 'Son of Cronos, neither the might of Athena nor of Ares can avail to deliver the Frogs from utter destruction. Rather, come and let us all go to help them, or else let loose your weapon, the great and formidable Titan-killer with which you killed Capaneus, that doughty man, and great Enceladus and the wild tribes of Giants; ay, let it loose, for so the most valiant will be slain.'

(ll. 285-293) So said Hera: and the Son of Cronos cast a lurid thunderbolt: first he thundered and made great Olympus shake, and then cast the thunderbolt, the awful weapon of Zeus, tossing it lightly forth. Thus he frightened them all, Frogs and Mice alike, hurling his bolt upon them. Yet even so the army of the Mice did not relax, but hoped still more to destroy the brood of warrior Frogs. Only, the Son of Cronos, on Olympus, pitied the Frogs and then straightway sent them helpers.

(ll. 294-303) So there came suddenly warriors with mailed backs and curving claws, crooked beasts that walked sideways, nut-cracker-jawed, shell-hided: bony they were, flat-backed, with glistening shoulders and bandy legs and stretching arms and eyes that looked behind them. They had also eight legs and two feelers—persistent creatures who are called crabs. These nipped off the tails and paws and feet of the Mice with their jaws, while spears only beat on them. Of these the Mice were all afraid and no longer stood up to them, but turned and fled. Already the sun was set, and so came the end of the one-day war.

Βατραχομυομαχία

—■◆■—

THE BATTLE OF THE FROGS AND MICE

Translated into English blank verse
during the Late Modern English period

by William Cowper

Published as part of his larger work
The Iliad and Odyssey of Homer
1791

—■◆■—

DESCEND all Helicon into my breast!
Oh ev'ry virgin of the tuneful choir
Breathe on my song which I have newly traced
In tables open'd on my knees, a song
Of bloodiest note—terrible deeds of Mars

5

Well worthy of the ears of all mankind,
Whom I desire to teach, how, erst, the Mice
Assail'd the Frogs, mimicking in exploit
The prowess of the giant race earth-born.
The rumour once was frequent in the mouths
                    10

Of mortal men, and thus the strife began.
A thirsty Mouse (thirsty with fear and flight
From a cat's claws) sought out the nearest lake,
Where, dipping in the flood his downy chin,
He drank delighted. Him the frog far-famed
                    15

[1]Limnocharis espied, and thus he spake.
Who art thou, stranger? Whence hast thou arrived
On this our border, and who gave thee birth?
Beware thou trespass not against the truth;
Lye not! for should I find thy merit such
                    20

As claims my love, I will conduct thee hence
To my abode, where gifts thou shalt receive
Lib'ral and large, with hospitable fare.
I am the King [2]Physignathus, revered
By the inhabitants of all this pool,
                    25

Chief of the frogs for ever. Me, long since,
[3]Peleus begat, embracing on the banks
Of the Eridanus my mother fair,
[4]Hydromedusa. Nor thee less than King
Or leader bold in sight thy form proclaims,
30

Stout as it is, and beautiful.—Dispatch—
Speak, therefore, and declare thy pedigree.
He ceas'd, to whom [5]Psycharpax thus replied,
Illustrious sir! wherefore hast thou enquired
My derivation, known to all, alike
35

To Gods and men, and to the fowls of heav'n?
I am Psycharpax, and the dauntless Chief
[6]Troxartes is my sire, whose beauteous spouse
Daughter of [7]Pternotroctes brought me forth,
[8]Lichomyle by name. A cave of earth
40

My cradle was, and, in my youngling state,
My mother nourish'd me with almonds, figs,
And delicacies of a thousand names.
But diverse as our natures are, in nought
Similar, how, alas! can we be friends?
45

The floods are thine abode, while I partake
With man his sustenance. The basket, stored
With wheaten loaves thrice kneaded, 'scapes not me,
Nor wafer broad, enrich'd with balmy sweets,
Nor ham in slices spread, nor liver wrapt
50

In tunic silver-white, nor curds express'd
From sweetest milk, nor, sweeter still, the full
Honeycomb, coveted by Kings themselves,
Nor aught by skilful cook invented yet
of sauce or seas'ning for delight of man.
55

I am brave also, and shrink not at sound
Of glorious war, but rushing to the van,
Mix with the foremost combatants. No fear
Of man himself shakes me, vast as he is,
But to his bed I steal, and make me sport
60

Nibbling his fingers' end, or with sharp tooth
Fretting his heel so neatly that he sleeps
Profound the while, unconscious of the bite.
Two things, of all that are, appall me most,
The owl and cat. These cause me many a pang.
65

As does the hollow gin insidious, fair
In promises, but in performance foul,
Engine of death! yet most of all I dread
Cats, nimble mousers, who can dart a paw
After me, enter at what chink I may,
                    70

But to return—your diet, parsley, kail,
Beet, radish, gourd, (for, as I understand,
Ye eat no other) are not to my taste.
Him then with smiles answer'd Physignathus.
Stranger! thou vauntest much thy dainty fare,
                    75

But, both on shore and in the lake, we boast
Our dainties also, and such fights as much
Would move thy wonder; for by gift from Jove
We leap as well as swim, can range the land
For food, or, diving, seek it in the Deep.
                    80

Would'st thou the proof? 'tis easy-mount my back
There cling as for thy life, and thou shalt share
With rapture the delights of my abode.
He said, and gave his back. Upsprang the mouse
Lightly, and with his arms enfolded fast
                    85

The Frog's soft neck. Pleas'd was he, at the first,
With view of many a creek and bay, nor less
With his smooth swimming on whose back he rode.
But when, at length, the clear wave dash'd his sides,
Then, fill'd with penitential sorrows vain

90

He wept, pluck'd off his hair, and gath'ring close
His hinder feet, survey'd with trembling heart
The novel sight, and wish'd for land again.
Groans follow'd next, extorted groans, through stress
Of shiv'ring fear, and, with extended tail

95

Drawn like a long oar after him, he pray'd
For land again; but, while he pray'd, again
The clear wave dash'd him. Much he shriek'd, and much
He clamour'd, and, at length, thus, sorrowing, said.
Oh desp'rate navigation strange! not thus

100

Europa floated to the shores of Crete
On the broad back of her enamour'd bull.
And now, dread spectacle to both, behold
An Hydra! on the lake with crest erect
He rode, and right toward them. At that sight

105

Down went Physignathus, heedless, alas!
Through fear, how great a Prince he should destroy.
Himself, at bottom of the pool escaped
The dreadful death; but, at his first descent
Dislodg'd, Psycharpax fell into the flood.
110

There, stretch'd supine, he clench'd his hands, he shriek'd,
Plunged oft, and, lashing out his heels afar,
Oft rose again, but no deliv'rance found.
At length, oppress'd by his drench'd coat, and soon
To sink for ever, thus he prophecied.
115

Thou hast releas'd thy shoulders at my cost,
Physignathus!, unfeeling as the rock,
But not unnoticed by the Gods above.
Ah worst of traytors! on dry land, I ween,
Thou hadst not soil'd me, whether in the race
120

Or wrestling-match, or at whatever game.
Thou hast by fraud prevail'd, casting me off
Into the waters; but an eye divine
Sees all. Nor hope thou to escape the host
Of Mice, who shall, ere long, avenge the deed.
125

So saying, he sank and died, whom, while he sat
Reposing on the lake's soft verge, the Mouse
[9]Lichopinax observed; aloud he wail'd,
And flew with those sad tidings to his friends.
Grief, at the sound, immeasurable seized
                    130

On all, and, by command, at dawn of day
The heralds call'd a council at the house
Of brave Troxartes, father of the Prince
Now lost, a carcase now, nor nigh to land
Welt'ring, but distant in the middle pool.
                    135

The multitude in haste convened, uprose
Troxartes for his son incensed, and said,
Ah friends! although my damage from the Frogs
Sustain'd be greatest, yet is yours not small.
Three children I have lost, wretch that I am,
                    140

All sons. A merciless and hungry cat
Finding mine eldest son abroad, surprized
And slew him. Lured into a wooden snare,
(New machination of unfeeling man
For slaughter of our race, and named a trap)
                    145

My second died. And now, as ye have heard,
My third, his mothers' and my darling, him
Physignathus hath drown'd in yon abyss.
Haste therefore, and in gallant armour bright
Attired, march forth, ye Mice, now seek the foe.
150

So saying, he roused them to the fight, and Mars
Attendant arm'd them. Splitting, first, the pods
Of beans which they had sever'd from the stalk
With hasty tooth by night, they made them greaves.
Their corslets were of platted straw, well lined
155

With spoils of an excoriated cat.
The lamp contributed its central tin,
A shield for each. The glitt'ring needle long
Arm'd ev'ry gripe with a terrific spear,
And auburn shells of nuts their brows inclosed.
160

Thus arm'd the Mice advanced, of whose approach
The Frogs apprized, emerging from the lake,
All throng'd to council, and consid'ring sat
The sudden tumult and its cause. Then came,
Sceptre in hand, an herald. Son was he
165

Of the renown'd [10]Tyroglyphus, and call'd
[11]Embasichytrus. Charged he came to announce
The horrors of approaching war, and said—
Ye Frogs! the host of Mice send you by me
Menaces and defiance, Arm, they say,
                    170

For furious fight; for they have seen the Prince
Psycharpax welt'ring on the waves, and drown'd
By King Physignathus. Ye then, the Chiefs
And leaders of the host of Frogs, put on
Your armour, and draw forth your bands to battle!
                    175

He said, and went. Then were the noble Frogs
Troubled at that bold message, and while all
Murmur'd against Physignathus, the King
Himself arising, thus denied the charge.
My friends! I neither drown'd the Mouse, nor saw
His drowning. Doubtless, while he strove in sport
                    181

To imitate the swimming of the Frogs,
He sank and died. Thus, blame is none in me,
And these injurious sland'rers do me wrong.
Consult we, therefore, how we may destroy
                    185

The subtle Mice, which thus we will perform.
Arm'd and adorn'd for battle, we will wait
Their coming where our coast is most abrupt.
Then, soon as they shall rush to the assault,
Seizing them by the helmet, as they come,
190

We will precipitate them, arms and all,
Into the lake; unskilful as they are
To swim, their suffocation there is sure,
And we will build a trophy to record
The great Mouse-massacre for evermore.
195

So saying, he gave commandment, and all arm'd.
With leaves of mallows [1] each his legs incased,
Guarded his bosom with a corslet cut
From the green beet, with foliage tough of kail
Fashion'd his ample buckler, with a rush
200

Keen-tipt, of length tremendous, fill'd his gripe,
And on his brows set fast a cockle-shell.
Then, on the summit of the loftiest bank
Drawn into phalanx firm they stood, all shook
Their quiv'ring spears, and wrath swell'd ev'ry breast.
Jove saw them, and assembling all the Gods
206

---

[1] Editor's Note: Mallow is the plant from which marshmallows used to be made (using the root sap).

To council in the skies, behold, he said,
Yon num'rous hosts, magnanimous, robust,
And rough with spears, how like the giant race
They move, or like the Centaurs! smiling, next,
210

He ask'd, of all the Gods, who favour'd most
The Mice, and who the Frogs? but, at the last,
Turning toward Minerva, thus he spake.
The Mice, my daughter, need thee; go'st thou not
To aid thy friends the Mice, inmates of thine,
215

Who to thy temple drawn by sav'ry steams
Sacrificial, and day by day refresh'd
With dainties there, dance on thy sacred floor?
So spake the God, and Pallas thus replied.
My father! suffer as they may, the Mice
220

Shall have no aid from me, whom much they wrong,
Marring my wreaths, and plund'ring of their oil
My lamps.—But this, of all their impious deeds,
Offends me most, that they have eaten holes
In my best mantle, which with curious art
225

Divine I wove, light, easy, delicate;
And now, the artificer whom I employ'd
To mend it, clamouring demands a price
Exorbitant, which moves me much to wrath,
For I obtain'd on trust those costly threads,
                    230

And have not wherewithal to pay th' arrear.
Nor love I more the Frogs, or purpose more
To succour even them, since they not less,
Dolts as they are, and destitute of thought,
Have incommoded[1] me. For when, of late,
                    235

Returning from a fight weary and faint
I needed rest, and would have slept, no sleep
Found I, those ceaseless croakers of the lake
Noisy, perverse, forbidding me a wink.
Sleepless, and with an aching head I lay
                    240

Therefore, until the crowing of the cock.
By my advice, then, O ye Gods, move not
Nor interfere, favouring either side,
Lest ye be wounded; for both hosts alike
Are valiant, nor would scruple[1] to assail
                    245

---

[1] Editor's Note: Incommode: to bother, inconvenience, disturb.

Even ourselves. Suffice it, therefore, hence
To view the battle, safe, and at our ease.
She ceas'd, and all complied. Meantime, the hosts
Drew nearer, and in front of each was seen
An herald, gonfalon in hand; huge gnats
250

Through clarions of unwieldy length sang forth
The dreadful note of onset fierce, and Jove
Doubled the signal, thund'ring from above.
First, with his spear [12]Hypsiboas assail'd
[13]Lichenor. Deep into his body rush'd
255

The point, and pierced his liver. Prone he fell,
And all his glossy down with dust defiled.
Then, [14]Troglodytes hurl'd his massy spear
At [15]Pelion, which he planted in his chest.
Down dropp'd the Frog, night whelm'd him, and he died.
[16]Seutlæus, through his heart piercing him, flew
261

Embasichytrus. [17]Polyphonus fell,
Pierced through his belly by the spear of bold
[18]Artophagus, and prone in dust expired.
Incensed at sight of Polyphonus slain,
265

---

[1] Editor's Note: Scruple: to be unwilling to do something because it is immoral or improper.

Limnocharis at Troglodytes cast
A mill-stone weight of rock; full on the neck
He batter'd him, and darkness veil'd his eyes.
At him Lichenor hurl'd a glitt'ring lance,
Nor err'd, but pierced his liver. Trembling fled
270

[19]Crambophagus at that dread sight, and plunged
Over the precipice into the lake,
Yet even there found refuge none, for brave
Lichenor following, smote him even there.
So fell Crambophagus, and from that fall
275

Never arose, but redd'ning with his blood
The wave, and wallowing in the strings and slime
Of his own vitals, near the bank expired.
[20]Limnisius on the grassy shore struck down
[21]Tyroglyphus; but at the view alone
280

Of terrible [22]Pternoglyphus appall'd,
Fled [23]Calaminthius, cast away his shield
Afar, and headlong plunged into the lake.
[24]Hydrocharis with a vast stone assail'd
The King [25]Pternophagus; the rugged mass
285

Descending on his poll, crush'd it; the brain
Ooz'd through this nostrils drop by drop, and all
The bank around was spatter'd with his blood.
Lichopinax with his long spear transpierced
[26]Borborocoites; darkness veil'd his eyes.
290

[27]Prassophagus with vengeful notice mark'd
[28]Cnissodioctes; seizing with one hand
His foot, and with the other hand his neck,
He plunged, and held him plunged, 'till, drown'd, he died.
Psycharpax standing boldly in defence
295

Of his slain fellow-warriors, urged his spear
Right through [29]Pelusius; at his feet he fell,
And, dying, mingled with the Frogs below.
Resentful of his death, the mighty Frog
[30]Pelobates an handful cast of mud
300

Full at Psycharpax; all his ample front
He smear'd, and left him scarce a glimpse of day.
Psycharpax, at the foul dishonour, still
Exasp'rate more, upheaving from the ground
A rock that had incumber'd long the bank,
305

Hurl'd it against Pelobates; below
The knees he smote him, shiver'd his right leg
In pieces, and outstretch'd him in the dust.
But him [31]Craugasides, who stood to guard
The fallen Chief, assail'd; with his long lance
310

He prick'd Psycharpax at the waist; the whole
Keen-pointed rush transpierced his belly, and all
His bowels following the retracted point,
O'erspread the ensanguin'd herbage at his side.
Soon as [32]Sitophagus, a crippled mouse,
315

That fight beheld, limping, as best he could,
He left the field, and, to avoid a fate
Not less tremendous, dropp'd into a ditch.
Troxartes grazed the instep of the bold
Physignathus, who at the sudden pang
320

Startled, at once leap'd down into the lake.
[33]Prassæus, at the sight of such a Chief
Floating in mortal agonies enraged,
Sprang through his foremost warriors, and dismiss'd
His pointed rush, but reach'd not through his shield
325

Troxartes, baffled by the stubborn disk.
There was a Mouse, young, beautiful, and brave
Past all on earth, son of the valiant Chief
[34]Artepibulus. Like another Mars
He fought, and [35]Meridarpax was his name,
                    330

A Mouse, among all Mice without a peer.
Glorying in his might on the lake's verge
He stood, with other Mouse none at his side,
And swore t' extirpate the whole croaking race.
Nor doubted any but he should perform
                    335

His dreadful oath, such was his force in arms,
Had not Saturnian Jove with sudden note
Perceived his purpose; with compassion touch'd
Of the devoted Frogs the Sov'reign shook
His brows, and thus the Deities address'd,
                    340

I see a prodigy, ye Pow'rs divine!
And, with no small amazement smitten, hear
Prince Meridarpax menacing the Frogs
With gen'ral extirpation. Haste—be quick—
Dispatch we Pallas terrible in sight,
                    345

Nor her alone, but also Mars, to quell
With force combined the sanguinary Chief.
So spake the Thund'rer, and thus Mars replied.
Neither the force of Pallas, nor the force
Of Mars, O Jove! will save the destin'd Frogs
350

From swift destruction. Let us all descend
To aid them, or, lest all suffice not, grasp
And send abroad thy biggest bolt, thy bolt
Tempestuous, terrour of the Titan race,
By which those daring enemies thou flew'st,
355

And didst coerce with adamantine[1] chains
Enceladus, and all that monstrous brood.
He said, and Jove dismiss'd the smould'ring bolt.
At his first thunder, to its base he shook
The vast Olympian. Then—whirling about
360

His forky fires, he launch'd them to the ground,
And, as they left the Sov'reign's hand, the heart
Of ev'ry Mouse quaked, and of ev'ry Frog.
Yet ceas'd not, even at that shock, the Mice
From battle, but with double ardour flew
365

---

[1] Editor's Note: Adamantine: quality of being adamant; unyielding; unbreakable.

To the destruction of the Frogs, whom Jove
From the Olympian heights snow-crown'd again
Viewing, compassionated their distress,
And sent them aids. Sudden they came. Broad-back'd
They were, and smooth like anvils, sickle-claw'd,
370

Sideling in gait, their mouths with pincers arm'd,
Shell-clad, crook-knee'd, protruding far before
Long hands and horns, with eye-balls in the breast,
Legs in quaternion ranged on either side,
And Crabs their name. They, seizing by his leg,
375

His arm, his tail a Mouse, cropp'd it, and snapp'd
His polish'd spear. Appall'd at such a foe
The miserable Mice stood not, but fled
Heartless, discomfited. [1] —And now, the sun
Descending, closed this warfare of a day.
380

THE END

---

[1] Editor's Note: Discomfited: embarrassed, uncomfortable.

Translator's End Notes

1. The beauty of the lake.
2. The pouter.
3. Of or belonging to mud.
4. Governess of the waters.
5. The crumb-catcher.
6. The bread-eater.
7. The bacon-eater.
8. The licker of mill-stones.
9. The dish-licker.
10. A cheese-rasper.
11. The explorer of pots and pipkins.
12. The loud-croaker.
13. One addicted to licking.
14. A creeper into holes and crannies.
15. Offspring of the mud.
16. A feeder on beet.
17. The noisy.
18. The bread-eater.
19. The cabbage-eater.
20. Of the lake.
21. The cheese-scraper.
22. The ham-scraper.
23. So called from the herb calamint.
24. One whose delight is in the water.
25. The bacon-eater.
26. The sleeper in the mud.

27. The garlic-eater.

28. The sav'ry-steam-hunter.

29. The muddy.

30. The mud-walker.

31. The hoarse-croaker.

32. The cake-eater.

33. One who deals much in garlic.

34. One who lies in wait for bread.

35. The scrap-catcher.

Βατραχομυομαχία

THE BATTLE OF THE FROGS AND MICE

Early Modern English Translation[1]

by George Chapman,

Included in a larger collection titled
The Crowne of all Homer's Workes.
1624

---

[1] Editor's Note: Early Modern English spelling can be challenging for new-comers. Some of the words spelled differently from Current English can be deciphered by reading the word or phrase aloud. If you still have trouble with a word, make note of it and of the sentence in which you found it. Often you will encounter the word again, and begin to understand its meaning in context. After reading the two previous translations, you will already be familiar with the story, and failing to catch the meaning of a few words will not detract from the pleasure of the reading.

The translator has provided extensive endnotes, and you will see from their content that he assumed the readers had abilities with Greek and Latin. Whether you do or not, it will be an amusing and enriching challenge to read this translation.

Entring the fields, first let my Vowes call on
The Muses whole Quire out of Helicon
Into my Heart; for such a Poems sake,
As lately I did in my Tables take,
And put into report, vpon my knees.
A fight so fierce, as might in all degrees
Fit Mars himselfe, and his tumultuous hand,
Glorying to dart to th'eares of euery land
Of all the a [1]voice-deuided; And to show
How brauely did both Froggs and Mise bestow
In glorious fight their forces; euen the deedes
Daring to imitate of earths Giant-seedes.
Thus then, men talkt; this seede the strife begat:

The Mouse, once drie; and scap't the dangerous Cat;
Drench't in the neighbour lake, her tender berde,
To taste the sweetnesse of the waue it rer'de.

The farre-fam'de Fen-affecter (seeing him) said;
Ho? Stranger? what are you? And whence, that tred
This shore of ours? who brought you forth? replie,
What truth may witnesse, lest I finde, you lie.
If worth fruition of my loue, and me;
Ile haue thee home; and Hospitalitie
Of feast, and gift; good and magnificent
Bestow on thee: For all this Confluent
Resounds my Royaltie; my Name, the great
In blowne-vp count'nances; and lookes of threat,
[2]Physignathus; ador'd of all Frogs here
All their daies durance; And the Empire beare

Of all their Beings. Mine owne Beeing, begot
By royall [3]Peleus; mixt in nuptiall knot,
With faire [4]Hydromedusa; On the Bounds
Nere which [5]Eridanus, his Race resounds.
And Thee, mine Eie, makes my Conceipt enclinde
To reckon powerfull, both in forme, and Minde:
A Scepter-bearer; And past others farre,
Aduanc't in all the fiery Fights of warre.
Come then, Thy race, to my renowne commend.
The Mouse made answer; why enquires my friend?
For what so well, know men and Deities,
And all the wing'd affecters of the skies?

[6]Psycharpax, I am calld; [7]Troxartes seede;
Surnam'de the Mighty-Minded: She that free'd
Mine eies from darknesse; was [8]Lichomyle,
King [9]Pternotroctes Daughter; shewing me
Within an aged houell, the young light:
Fed me with figges, and nuts; and all the height
Of varied viands. But vnfolde the cause,
Why, 'gainst similitudes most equall lawes
(Obseru'd in friendship) thou makst me thy friend?
Thy life, the waters only helpe t'extend.
Mine, whatsoeuer, men are vs'd to eat,
Takes part with them, at shore: their purest cheat,
Thrice boulted, kneaded, and subdu'd in past]],
In cleane round kymnels; cannot be so fast
From my approches kept; but in I eat:
Nor Cheesecakes full, of finest Indian wheat,
That [10]Crustie-weedes weare, large as Ladies traines:

[11] Lyurings, (white-skind as Ladies:) nor the straines
Of prest milke, renneted; Nor collups cut,
Fresh from the flitch: Nor iunkets such as put
Palats diuine in Appetite: nor any
Of all mens delicates; thought ne're so many
Their Cookes deuise them, who each dish see deckt
With all the dainties[12] all strange soiles affect.
Yet am I not so sensuall, to flie
Of fields embattaild, the most fiery crie:
But rush out strait; and with the first in sight,
Mixe in aduenture: No man with affright
Can daunt my forces; though his bodie bee
Of neuer so immense a quantitie.
But making vp, euen to his bed, accesse;
His fingers ends dare with my teeth compresse:
His feet taint likewise; and so soft sease both,
They shall not tast Th'Impression of a tooth.

Sweet sleepe shall holde his owne, in euery eie
Where my tooth takes his tartest libertie:
But two there are, that alwaies, far and neare
Extremely still, controule my force with feare;
(The Cat, and Night-Hawke) who much skathe confer
On all the Outraies, where for food I erre.
Together with the [13]streights-still-keeping Trap;
Where lurkes deceiptfull and set-spleend Mishap.
But most of all the Cat constraines my feare;
Being euer apt t'assault me euery where:
For by that hole, that hope saies, I shall scape,
At that hole euer, she commits my Rape.

The best is yet, I eat no pot-herb grasse,
Nor Raddishes; nor Coloquintida's:
Nor Still-greene; Beetes, nor Parsley: which you make
Your dainties still, that liue vpon the lake.
The Frog replide: Stranger? your boasts creepe all
Vpon their bellies; though to our liues fall;
Much more miraculous meates, by lake and land:
Ioue tendring our liues with a twofold hand;
Enabling vs to leape ashore for food,
And hide vs strait in our retreatfull flood:
Which if your will serue; you may proue with ease.
Ile take you on my shoulders: which fast sease,
If safe arriuall at my house y'intend.

He stoopt; and thither spritelie did ascend,
Clasping his golden necke, that easie seat
Gaue to his sallie: who was iocund yet;
Seeing the safe harbors of the King so nere;
And he, a swimmer so exempt from Pere.
But when he sunke into the purple waue;
He mournd extremely; and did much depraue
Vnprofitable penitence: His haire
Tore by the roots vp, labord for the aire,
With his feet fetcht vp to his belly, close:
His heart within him, panted out repose,
For th'insolent plight, in which his state did stand:
Sigh'd bitterly, and long'd to greete the land,
Forc't by the dire Neede, of his freezing feare.
First on the waters, he his taile did stere
Like to a Sterne: then drew it like an ore,

Still praying the Gods to set him safe ashore:
Yet sunke he midst the red waues, more and more,
And laid a throat out, to his vtmost height:
Yet in forc'd speech, he made his perill sleight;
And thus his glorie with his grieuance stroue;

Not in such choice state was the charge of loue
Borne by the Bull; when to the Cretane shore
He swumme Europa through the wauie rore;
As this Frog ferries me; His pallid brest
Brauely aduancing; and his verdant crest
(Submitted to my seat) made my support,
Through his white waters, to his royall Court.
But on the sudden did apparance make
An horrid spectacle; a water-snake
Thrusting his freckeld necke aboue the lake.
Which (seene to both) away Physignathus
Diu'd to his deepes; as no way conscious
Of whom, he left to perish in his lake;
But shunn'd blacke fate himselfe; and let him take
The blackest of it: who amids the Fenn
Swumme with his brest vp; hands held vp in vaine,
Cried Peepe, and perisht: sunke the waters oft,
And often with his sprawlings, came aloft;
Yet no way kept downe deaths relentlesse force:
But (full of water) made an heauie Corse.
Before he perisht yet, he threatned thus;

Thou lurk'st not yet from heauen (Physignathus)
Though yet thou hid'st here, that hast cast from thee
    (As from a Rocke,) the shipwrackt life of mee.
    Though thou thy selfe, no better was than I
        (O worst of things) at any facultie;
        Wrastling or race: but for thy perfidie
In this my wracke; Ioue beares a wreakefull eie:
And to the Hoast of Mise, thou paines shalt pay
        Past all euasion. This, his life let say,
    And left him to the waters. Him beheld,

    [14]Lichopinax; plac't in the pleasing fielde:
Who shrick't extremely; ranne and told the Mise;
        Who, hauing heard his watry destinies;
        Pernicious anger pierst the hearts of all;
    And then their Heralds, forth they sent to call
        A councell early, at Troxartes house,
        Sad father of this fatall shipwrack't Mouse:
Whose dead Corpse, vpwards swum along the lake;
Nor yet (poore wretch) could be enforc'd to make
    The shore, his harbour; but the mid-Maine swum:
When now (all haste made) with first morne did come
    All to set councell; in which, first rais'd head,
        Troxartes, angrie for his sonne; and said;

    O Friends, though I alone may seeme to beare
        All the infortune; yet may all mette here
        Account it their case. But tis true, I am

In chiefe vnhappy; that a triple flame
Of life, feele put forth, in three famous sonnes;
The first, the chiefe in our confusions
(The Cat) made rape of; caught without his hole:
The second; Man, made with a cruell soule,
Brought to his ruine, with a new-found sleight;
And a most woodden engine of deceipt,
They terme a Trap; mere [15]Murthresse of our Mise.
The last that in my loue held speciall prise,
And his rare mothers; this Physignathus
(With false pretext of wafting to his house;)
Strangl'd in chiefe deepes, of his bloudy streame.
Come then; haste all, and issue out on them,
Our bodies deckt, in our Dedalean armes.
This said; his words thrust all vp in alarmes;
And Mars himselfe, that serues the cure of war;
Made all in their Appropriats circular.
First on each leg, the greene shales of a Beane,
They clos'd for Bootes; that sat [16]exceeding cleane:
The shales they broke ope, Bootehaling by night,
And eat the beanes: Their Iacks; Art exquisite
Had showne in them; being Cats-skins, euery where
Quilted with quills: Their fencefull bucklers were,
The middle rounds of Can'sticks; but their speare
A huge long Needle was; that could not beare
The braine of any; but be Mars his owne
Mortall inuention. Their heads arming Crowne
Was vessel to the kirnell of a nut:
And thus the Mise, their powers in armour put.

This, the frogs hearing; From the water, all
Issue to one place; and a councell call
Of wicked war; consulting what should be
Cause to this murmure, and strange mutinie.
While this was question'd; neere them made his stand
An Herald with a Scepter in his hand,
([17]Embasichytrus calld) that fetcht his kinde,
From [18]Tyroglyphus, with the mightie minde;
Denouncing ill-nam'd war, in these high termes;

O Frogs? the Mise, sends threats to you of armes
And bid me bid ye Battell; and fixt fight;
Their eies all wounded with Psycharpax sight,
Floting your waters, whom your king hath kild.
And therefore all prepare for force of field,
You that are best borne, whosoeuer held.
This said; he seuer'd; his speech firing th'eares
Of all the Mise; but frees'd the Frogs with feares,
Themselues conceiting guiltie; whom the King
Thus answer'd (rising.) Friends? I did not bring
Psycharpax to his end; He, wantoning
Vpon our waters, practising to swimme,
[19]Ap'te vs, and drown'd; without my sight of him.
And yet these worst of Vermine, accuse me
Though no way guiltie. Come, consider we
How we may ruine these deceiptfull Mise.
For my part; I giue voice to this aduise;
As seeming fittest to direct our deeds.
Our bodies decking with our arming weeds;

Let all our Powr's stand rais'd in steep'st repose
Of all our shore; that when they charge vs close;
We may the helms snatch off, from all so deckt,
Daring our onset; and them all direct
Downe to our waters. Who not knowing the sleight
To diue our soft deeps, may be strangl'd streight;
And we triumphing, may a Trophey rere,
Of all the Mise, that we haue slaughter'd here.

These words put all in armes; and mallow leaues
They drew vpon their leggs, for arming [20]Greaues.
Their Curets; broad greene Beetes; their bucklers were
Good thick-leau'd Cabbadge; proofe gainst any spe're.
Their speares, sharpe Bullrushes; of which, were all
Fitted with long ones. Their parts Capitall
They hid in subtle Cockleshels from blowes.
And thus, all arm'd; the steepest shores they chose,
T'encamp themselues; where lance with lance, they lin'd;
And brandisht brauelie; each Frogg full of Minde.

Then Ioue calld all Gods, in his flaming Throne
And shewd all, all this preparation
For resolute warre. These able soldiers,
Many, and great; all shaking lengthfull spe'res:
In shew like Centaures; or the Gyants Host.
When (sweethe smiling,) he enquir'd who, most
Of all th'Immortalls, pleas'd to adde their aide
To Froggs or Mise: and thus to Pallas said;

O daughter? Must not you, needs aid these Mise?
That with the Odors, and meate sacrifice
Vs'd in your Temple, endlesse triumphs make;
And serue you, for your sacred victles sake?

Pallas repli'd; O Father, neuer I
Will aid the Mise, in anie miserie.
So many mischiefes by them, I haue found;
[21]Eating the Cotten, that my distaffs crown'd;
My lamps still banting, to deuoure the oyle.
But that which most my minde eates, is their spoile
Made of a veile, that me in much did stand:
On which, bestowing an elaborate hand;
A fine woofe working; of as pure a thredd;
Such holes therein, their Petulancies fed;
That, putting it to darning; when't'was done;
The darner, a most deare paie stood vpon
For his so deare paines; laid downe instantlie;
[22]Or (to forbeare) exacted vsurie.
So, borrowing from my Phane, the weed I woue;
I can by no meanes, th'vsurous darner, moue
To let me haue the mantle to restore.
And this is it, that rubs the angrie sore
Of my offence tooke, at these petulant Mise.
Nor will I yeeld, the Froggs wants, my supplies,
For their infirme mindes; that no confines keepe;
For I, from warre retir'd; and wanting sleepe;
All lept ashore in tumult; nor would staie

Till one winck seas'd myne eyes: and so I laie
Sleeplesse, and pain'de with headach; till first light
The Cock had crow'd vp. Therefore, to the fight
Let no God goe assistent; lest a lance
Wound whosoeuer offers to aduance;
Or wishes but their aid; that skorne all foes;
Should any Gods accesse, their spirits oppose.
Sit we then pleas'd, to see from heauen, their fight.

She said; and all Gods ioin'd in her delight.
And now, both Hosts, to one field drew the iarre;
Both Heralds bearing the ostents of warre.
And then the [23]wine-Gnats, that shrill Trumpets sound
Terriblie rung out, the encounter, round.
Ioue thundred; all heauen, sad warrs signe resounded.

And first, [24]Hypsiboas,[25]Lychenor wounded,
Standing th'impression of the first in fight.
His lance did, in his Lyuers midsts alight,
Along his bellie. Downe he fell; his face,
His fall on that part swaid; and all the grace
Of his soft hayre, fil'd with disgracefull dust.

Then [26]Troglodytes, his thick iaueline thrust
In [27]Pelions bosome; bearing him to ground:
Whom sad death seas'd; his soule flew through his wound.

[28]Sentlæus next, Embasichytros slew;
His heart through thrusting: then [29]Artophagus threw

His lance at [30]Polyphon; and strooke him quite
Through his midd-bellie: downe he fell vpright:
And from his fayre limms, took his soule her flight.

[31]Lymnocharis beholding Polyphon
Thus done to death; did with as round a stone
As that the mill turnes; Troglodytes wound
Neare his mid-neck; ere he his onset found:
Whose eyes, sad darknes seas'd. [32]Lychenor cast
A flying dart off, and his ayme so plac't
Vpon Lymnocharis; that [33] Sure he thought
The wound he wisht him: nor vntruely wrought
The dire successe; for through his Lyuer flew
The fatall lance; which when [34]Crambaphagus knew;
Downe the deepe waues neare shore; he, diuing, fled;
But fled not fate so; the sterne enimie fed
Death with his life in diuing: neuer more
The ayre he drew in; his Vermilian gore
Staind all the waters; and along the shore
He lay extended; his fat entrailes laie
(By his small guts impulsion) breaking waie
Out at his wound. [35]Lymnisius, neare the shore
Destroid Tyroglyphus: which frighted sore
The soule of [36]Calaminth; seeing comming on
(For wreake) [37]Pternoglyphus: who got him gon

With large leapes to the lake; his Target throwne
Into the waters. [38]Hydrocharis slew
King [39]Pternophagus, at whose throte he threw

A huge stone; strooke it high; and beate his braine
Out at his nostrills: earth blusht, with the staine
His blood made on her bosom. For next Prise;
Lichopinax, to death did sacrifice
[40]Borborocœtes faultlesse faculties;
His lance enforc't it; darknes clos'd his eyes.
On which when [41]Brassophagus, cast his looke;
[42]Cnisodioctes, by the heeles he tooke;
Dragg'd him to fenn, from off his natiue ground;
Then seas'd his throte, and souc't him, till he droun'd.

But now; Psycharpax wreakes his fellows deaths;
And in the bosome of [43]Pelusius sheathes,
(In center of his Lyuer) his bright lance:
He fel before the Author of the chance;
His soule to hell fled. Which [44]Pelobates
Taking sad note of; wreakefully did sease
His hands gripe full of mudd; and all besmear'd;
His forhead with it so; that scarce appeard
The light to him. Which certainely incenst
His fierie splene: who, with his wreake dispenst
No point of tyme; but rer'd with his strong hand
A stone so massie, it opprest the land;
And hurld it at him; when, below the knee
It strooke his right legge so impetuouslie;
It peece-meale brake it; be the dust did sease,

Vpwards euerted. But [45]Craugasides
Reuendg'd his death; and at his enimie

Dischardg'd a dart; that did his point implie
In his mid-bellie. All the sharp-pil'de speare
Got after in; and did before it beare
His vniuersall entrailes to the earth,
Soone as his swolne hand, gaue his iaueline birth.

[46]Sitophagus, beholding the sad sight,
Set on the shore; went halting from the fight,
Vext with his wounds extremelie. And to make
Waie from extreme fate, lept into the lake.

Troxartes strooke, in th'insteps vpper part,
Physignathus; who, (priuie to the smart
His wound imparted) with his vtmost hast
Lept to the lake, and fled. Troxartes cast
His eye vpon the foe that fell before;
And, (see'ng him halfe-liu'de) long'd againe to gore
His gutlesse bosome; and (to kill him quite)
Ranne fiercely at him. Which [47]Prassæus sight
Tooke instant note of; and the first in fight
Thrust desp'rate way through; casting, his keene lance
Off at Troxartes; whose shield turn'd th'aduance
The sharpe head made: & checkt the mortall chance.

Amongst the Mise fought, an Egregiouse
Young spring all; and a close-encountring Mouse:
Pure [48]Artepibulus his deare descent:
A Prince that Mars himselfe shewd, where he went
(Call'd [49]Meridarpax.) Of so huge a might;

That onely He still, dominer'd in fight,
Of all the Mouse-Host. He aduancing close
Vp to the Lake; past all the rest arose
In glorious obiect; and made vant that He
Came to depopulate all the progenie
Of Froggs, affected with the lance of warre.
And certainely; he had put on as farre
As he aduanc't his vant; (he was indude
With so vnmatcht a force, and fortitude)
Had not the Father, both of Gods and Men
Instantly knowne it; and the Froggs (euen then
Giuen vp to ruine) rescude with remorse.
Who, (his head mouing,) thus began discourse:

No meane amaze, affects me to behold
Prince Meridarpax, rage so vncontrold,
In thirst of Frogg-blood; all along the lake:
Come therefore still; and all addression make;
Dispatching Pallas, with tumultuous Mars,
Downe to the field, to make him leaue the wars:
How [50]Potently soeuer he be said,
Where he attempts once; to vphold his head.

Mars answered; O Ioue; neither she nor I
(With both our aides) can keepe depopulacie
From off the Froggs. And therefore arme we all;
Euen thy lance letting brandish to his call
From off the field: that from the field withdrew

The Titanois; the Titanois that slew;
Though most exempt from match, of all earths seedes

So great and so inaccessible deeds
It hath proclaim'd to men; bound hand and foot,
The vast Enceladus; and rac't by th'root
The race of vpland Gyants. This speech past;
Saturnius, a smoking lightening cast
Amongst the armies; thundring then so sore,
That with a rapting circumflexe, he bore
All huge heauen ouer. But the terrible ire,
Of his dart, sent abroad, all wrapt in fire,
(Which certainely, his very finger was)
Amazde both Mise and Froggs. Yet soone let passe
Was all this by the Mise: who, much the more;
Burnd in desire t'exterminate the store
Of all those lance-lou'd souldiers. Which, had beene;
If, from Olympus, Ioues eye had not seene
The Froggs with pittie; and with instant speede
Sent them assistents. Who (ere any heede
Was giuen to their approch) came crawling on
With [51]Anuiles on their backs; that (beat vpon
Neuer so much) are neuer wearied, yet:
Crook-pawd; and wrested on, with foule clouen feet:
[52]Tongues in their mouths: Brick-backt, all ouer bone,
Broade-shoulderd; whence a ruddie yellow shone.
Distorted, and small thigh'd: had eyes that saw
Out at their bosomes. Twice foure feet did draw
About their bodies. Strong neckt; whence did rise

Two heads; nor could to any hand be Prise.
They call them Lobsters; that eat from the Mise,
Their tailes; their feet; and hands; and wrested all
Their lances from them so; that cold Appall
The wretches put in rout, past all returne.
And now the Fount of light forbore to burne
Aboue the earth. When (which mens lawes commend)
Our Battaile, in one daie, tooke absolute end.

The end of Homers Battaile of Frogges and Mise.

———◆——

Translator's Endnotes

1. (Intending men: being divided from all other creatures
   by the voice, ωεροψ, being a periphrasis, signifying voce
   divisus, of μειρω divido, and οψ οπὸς vox.)
2. Φυσιγναθος, Genas & buccas inflans.
3. Πηλεύς, qui ex luto nascitur.
4. Ύδρομέδυσα. Aquarum regina.
5. The river Po, in Italy.
6. Ψυχάρπαξ. Gather-crum, or lavish-crum.
7. Shear-crust.

8. Lick-mill.

9. Bacon-flitch-devourer, or gnawer.

10. Τανυπεπλος Extenso & promisso Peplo amictus. A metaphor taken from ladies veiles, or trains, and therefore their names are here added.

11. Ηπατα λευκοχὶτωνα Livering puddings white skin'd.

12. Παντοδαποῖσιν. Whose common exposition is only carijs, when it properly signifies, ex omni solo.

13. Στενόεσσαν, of στενος, Augustus.

14. Lick-dish.

15. Ολείτειρα interfectrix perditrix.

16. Ευ τ᾽ ἀσκήσαντες ab ασκεα elaborate concinno.

17. Enter-pot, or Search-pot.

18. Cheese-miner. Qui caseum rodendo cavat.

19. Μιμουμενος Aping or imitating us.

20. Boots of warre.

21. Στέμματα, Lavas, eo quad colus cingant seu coronent. Which our learned sect translate eating the crowns that Pallas wore.

22. Τόκος, Partus, et id quod partu edidit mater. Metap. hìc appellatur fœnus quod ex usurâ ad nos redit.

23. Κώνωφ. culex vinarius.

24. Loud-mouth.

25. Kitchen-vessel licker.

26. Hole-dweller, Qui foramina subit.

27. Mud-borne.

28. Beet-devourer.

29. The great bread-eater.

30. The great Noise maker, shrill or bigg-voic'd.

31. The lake-louer.

32. Qui lambit culinaria vasa.

33. Τιτύσκομαι intentissime dirigo, ut certum ictum inferam.

34. The cabbage-eater.

35. Paludis incola. Lake-liuer.

36. Qui in calaminthâ, herbâ palustri habitat.

37. Bacon-eater.

38. Qui Aquis delectatur.

39. Collup-deuourer.

40. Mudd-sleeper.

41. Leeke or scallion louer.

42. Kitchin smell haunter, or hunter.

43. Fenstalker.

44. Qui per lutum it.

45. Vociferator.

46. Eate-corne.

47. Scallian-deuourer.

48. Bread-betraier.

49. Scrap or broken-meat-eater.

50. Κρατερός validus seu potens in retinendo.

51. Νωτακμονες Incudes ferentes, or anvil backed. Ἀκμωε. Incus, dicta per sycopen, quasi nullis ictibus fatigetur.

52. Ψαλιδοστμοις Forcipem in ore habens.

IMAGE CITATIONS

In Order of Appearance

FRONT COVER: *The Abduction of Helen.* By Gavin Hamilton, c. 1770s. Image Public domain.

The Abduction of Helen. By R. von Deutsch, Reproduced in *Character Sketches*, Vol. III., by The Rev E. Cobham Brewer, 1901. From the editor's private collection.

Title Page from Chapman's Translation of Homer. Published by Nathaniel Butler, c. 1616. George Chapman lived 1515 - 1634 and was a classical scholar, English dramatist, poet, and translator.

Heinrich Schliemann. c. 1860. Фото Генриха Шлимана в 38 лет. 2008. Журнал "100 человек, которые изменили ход истории." Uniphoto Press. Public domain via Wikimedia.

Mask of Agamemnon. Funeral mask also known as "Agamemnon Mask." Gold, found in Tomb V in Mycenae by Heinrich Schliemann (1876), XVIth century BC. National Archeological Museum, Athens. 2 April 2005. DieBuche. Public domain, via Wikimedia.

Location Map of Greece. United States National Imagery and Mapping Agency. Lencer.23 July 2008. Public domain via Wikimedia. Edited by Allison Ellis to indicate approximate location of ancient Troy.

Homerus Venetus A. Homer. *Iliad*, Book II, lines 681–685. From the Codex Marcianus Graecus 454 (now 822) also known as Venetus A. 10th century.
https://www.internetculturale.it/jmms/iccuviewer/iccu.jsp?id=oai%3A1 93.206.197.121%3A18%3AVE0049%3ACSTOR.240.10164.
Public domain, via Wikimedia Commons.

Mykonos Vase (Archaeological Museum of Mykonos, Inv. 2240). Decorated pithos found at Mykonos, Greece depicting one of the earliest known renditions of the Trojan Horse. 670 B.C. Submitted by: Beyond My Kim. Public domain via Wikimedia Commons.

First page of the *Batrachomyomachia*, 1726. Public Domain via Wikimedia Commons.

LIST OF ILLUSTRATIONS from *The Iliad For Boys and Girls: Told in Simple Language*. Alfred J. Church. Originally published in 1907. Illustrations (uncredited) from the 1929 edition by The MacMillan Company, from the editor's private collection:

Athene Suppressing the Fury of Achilles

Diomed Casting His Spear Against Ares

Hector Chiding Paris

The Meeting of Hector and Andromache

Hector and Ajax Separated by the Heralds

Hera and Athene Going to Assist the Greeks

The Embassy of Achilles

Diomed and Ulysses Returning with the Spoils of Rhesus

Polydamus Advising Hector to Retire from the Trench

Ajax Defending the Greek Ships against the Trojans

Sleep and Death Conveying the Body of Sarpedon to Lycia

The Fight for the Body of Patroclus

The Gods Descending to Battle

Andromache Fainting on the Wall

Hector's Body Dragged by the Chariot of Achilles

MOUNT TITANO
MEDIA

Mount Titano Media publishes single works and collections of the greatest spoken and written words of all time in the fields of history, literature, poetry, philosophy, and politics for the benefit of families, schools, colleges, universities, and independent lovers of learning and culture.

Mount Titano Media Classical Studies Editions offer unique compilations of supplemental material to help readers understand the work's place within "The Great Conversation"—

MOUNT TITANO MEDIA
CLASSICAL STUDIES EDITION

or, the great works of Western Civilization—which leads back to the roots of our Judeo-Christian/Greco-Roman heritage.

To discuss anything in this book, please e-mail:
inquiry@mounttitanomedia.com

To become a distributor or retailer, please e-mail:
orders@mounttitanomedia.com

Schools, churches, civic organizations, book clubs, and individuals can purchase bulk orders at discounted prices. Bulk orders are nonreturnable. Please e-mail: sales@mounttitanomedia.com

— ALSO FROM MOUNT TITANO MEDIA—

Available in paperback, hardcover, and Kindle on Amazon.
For distribution and bulk orders, contact:

orders@mounttitanomedia.com

FINDING OUR WORDS
Words That Made America

FINDING OUR WORDS: Words That Made America is a collection of some of the most inspiring words spoken by American leaders since our founding, with every speech launched with a prefacing essay by Tracy Lee Simmons, acclaimed journalist and author of *Climbing Parnassus*, a popular case for classical education in America. In the essays, Simmons shows how each speech fits into the broad mosaic of the American story. Commerce with these words offers us one path back to citizenship, decency, and good sense.

FOR ALL AGES: For advanced readers to enjoy in leisure learning and for education at all levels. The book may be used exclusively or in conjunction with other works for the study of language arts, U.S. history, civics, statesmanship, and elocution. Included is a "Letter to the Reader" by Mount Titano Media founder Allison Ellis, which offers guidance for reading this and all great books with children and students of any age.

Available in paperback, hardcover, and Kindle on Amazon.
For distribution and bulk orders, contact:

orders@mounttitanomedia.com

HEROINES OF HISTORY

In this collection of stories from Greco-Roman antiquity to World War I, we meet a wide range of brave and faithful women, from keepers of the hearth to leaders of empire. They are presented in legend and mythology, poetry and essays, and true stories and letters. In these pages a wide array of history's heroines, some better known than others, come to life to admonish when we stray, console when we despair, and embolden when we falter.

These heroines are the mothers, wives, and friends whom we wish our young girls to emulate and our strong young sons to marry. They are women, in contrast to most popular culture figures, with the character and spirit we wish to see in all levels of leadership—domestic, professional, or otherwise.

Equally important in reading and learning, the stories of these heroines are told with uncommonly beautiful use of language.

FOR ALL AGES: For advanced readers to enjoy in leisure learning and for education at all levels. The book may be used exclusively or in conjunction with other works for the study of language arts, U.S. history, civics, statesmanship, and elocution. Included is a "Letter to the Reader" by Mount Titano Media founder Allison Ellis, which offers guidance for reading this and all great books with children and students of any age.

Available in paperback and hardcover on Amazon.
For distribution and bulk orders, contact:

orders@mounttitanomedia.com

QUO VADIS:
A Novel of the Time of Nero & the Early Church

CLASSICAL STUDIES EDITION

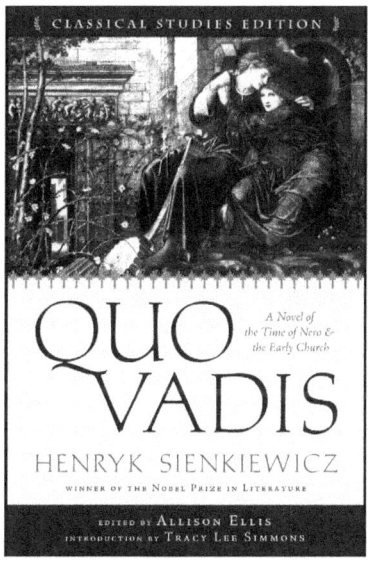

• Introduction by Tracy Lee Simmons, M.A., Classics, Oxford University, author of *Climbing Parnassus: A New Apologia for Greek and Latin*

• Reading Guide by Allison Ellis, founder of Mount Titano Media, for individuals and parents/teachers

• Reader Resource: *Roman Culture & Civilization* by Memoria Press, which includes maps of ancient Rome, Latin vocabulary, and an introduction to Roman mythology, culture, government, and everyday life

• Glossary of Latin terms found in the text and select images from antiquarian editions of *Quo Vadis*

• Lightly edited throughout for use in schools without compromising plot, character development, or meaning

"I know of no story better than Quo Vadis *to drive our young adults away from relationship as 'mutual use and abuse' and into relationship built on the founding Christian principle: 'My Life for Yours.'"*

—*Allison Ellis, Editor*

— **COMING SOON** —

MOUNT TITANO MEDIA
CLASSICAL STUDIES EDITION

www.ingramcontent.com/pod-product-compliance
Lightning Source LLC
Chambersburg PA
CBHW060948030726
47503CB00003B/785